Don't I Know You?

Anne Brooksbank

2024

A catalogue record for this
book is available from the
National Library of Australia

Title: Don't I Know You?
Publisher: Noisy Press
ISBN: 978-0-9924998-6-0 : Printed - Paperback
Date of Publication: September 2024

Editors: Simone Ford & Jack Ellis
Cover photo: Adelaide River, Wet Season, by Janelle
Cover design and typesetting by Jack Ellis

To Jane O'Keefe, with love

1

It was early in the morning, around six am, when Meg was woken by a loud knocking. Male voices yelled that she had to open up or they'd break the door down. She opened it thinking they must have the wrong house, but then a police officer handed her a warrant. It appeared that Nick, her thirty-one-year-old son, had been engaged in some transactions on the dark web and had used her name and her computer. The same officer demanded that she tell them where her son was, but she could only show them his room, where the bed hadn't been slept in, and say she had no idea. She stood by while they searched his messy room, apparently finding nothing. They went out to the backyard and a young constable asked for a key to the padlock on the shed.

Meg shook her head. 'My son has the key.'

He shrugged it off. 'It doesn't matter. We've got a bolt cutter.'

For a moment she wanted to laugh. Of course they had a bolt cutter and would use it in the same cheery, offhand way. The shed had been her husband Leon's private space and Nick had taken it over when he died. She felt physical pain as the police broke the lock and went inside.

After ten minutes or so they came out.

'Did you find anything?' she asked.

'We can't discuss that with you,' the older man told her. 'We need to talk to your son.'

Meg heard a note of frustration in his voice. It made her think that they hadn't found anything in the shed. His impatience was clear as he instructed two of the younger constables to dig up the garden beds. She might have protested but she knew there was no point. She watched in silence while they dug up and flattened many of the plants she'd cared for over the years, but nothing was found other than a Donald Duck toy. It had gone missing when Nick was a toddler. The same young constable who'd spoken to her before attempted to straighten several of the upturned plants, but they flopped over straightaway.

He smiled at her ruefully. 'Sorry.'

She didn't answer him. What was there to say?

He looked at her more closely. 'You're a doctor, aren't you?'

'Yes, I am.'

'My mother used to come and see you. She was sorry when you retired. She doesn't much like the one who came after you. You gave her more time.'

He apologised once more and left.

Meg drank two cups of coffee at the kitchen table before Nick came home. She told him about the police raid and the partial destruction of the backyard.

He went to the window to check the damage. 'I can fix that.'

'No, you can't uproot plants and then replant them. They're like people. It doesn't work.'

Nick ignored this. He went out and tried to straighten some of the plants, putting in a stake here and there for support, but he had little more success than the constable. Meg called him back into the kitchen and he came in warily.

'We have to talk about this,' she told him.

She watched him while he made a cup of coffee. He was thirty-one but looked younger because of his slim build, untidy dark-blond hair and a way of moving about that seemed to her much the same as when he was seventeen. He was just over six feet with good looks, warm brown eyes and an attentive expression that helped him in what appeared to be his plan to take life easily.

He sat down at the table with his coffee. 'Okay, go.'

She told him about the raid and demanded to know what had led to it. 'And don't lie to me. I have to know what we're up against.'

He gave her a quick smile. 'The "we" sounds promising.'

Meg stared back at him.

He sighed. 'I sold a few things on the dark web. Everyone does.'

'Do they? And you used my computer?'

He shrugged. 'I need a new laptop.'

Her tone was very cold. 'So what did you sell?'

'A few things from your medical bag.'

She was shocked. 'What things?'

He named several opioids.

Meg was becoming increasingly appalled. 'And you got paid for them?'

'Fifty bucks each. I needed a bit of cash.'

'But you know it's illegal, don't you? And the police think I did it.'

He smiled at her – the warm smile of his that she had always loved. 'Then I'll be a character witness for you in court. Can I go to bed now?'

Meg felt too tired to argue. 'This is not the end of it, you know.'

'I know.'

She went back to bed but couldn't sleep. She tried to read but found it too hard to concentrate. Later the same morning she heard Nick moving about the kitchen, presumably getting himself some breakfast. She went out and found him at the kitchen table eating the sandwich he'd made for himself. He looked at her in a sleepy, puzzled way as she sat down opposite.

'Will you go and talk to the cops about all this?' she asked, trying to keep her voice neutral.

He shook his head. 'They went to the trouble of getting a warrant. That means they were looking for something more than a few pills sold on the dark web.'

'So?'

'They'd need some real evidence and they didn't find any.'

'Are you sure of that?'

'Yeah, I'm sure.'

This confirmed her own impression that the cops had gone away annoyed by the apparent waste of their time.

Nick seemed more awake now. 'Someone could've dobbed me in, you know.'

'What do you mean?'

'Like someone in trouble with them did a deal. Gave them information.'

'So what?'

'The info they were given just happened to be a dud.'

'Who'd do that?'

'No idea.'

Meg suspected that he did in fact have some idea, but it wasn't likely that she'd get any more out of him. All of this wasn't new, but it was the first time the police had been involved. Nick had been going away and coming back unexpectedly ever since he left school. His final marks had been low but were good enough for him to take a bridging course and then get into university or TAFE. Both Meg and Leon had urged him to do that and had said they'd support him, but he claimed he was sick of studying and wanted a year off. She hadn't blamed him for it. It made sense at the time.

It started as just a break, but it lengthened. One year, two years, then more. He'd get a job but then argue with those above him, and sooner or later he'd either be fired or feel so bored that he'd quit. He started several small businesses that looked promising, but then things fell apart, often in ways not his fault, like an established competitor moving in nearby. He'd give up and come home and would sleep in his old room, working on further schemes. Most of them involved buying and selling but never seemed to bring in much return for his efforts. Meg thought he worked quite a lot harder at all this than he would have if he'd just had a job.

She watched him as he finished his breakfast, then asked abruptly, 'You're not scamming anyone, are you?'

He looked startled. 'What? No, of course I'm not.'

'No old ladies like me?'

'I don't think of you as an old lady.'

'Isn't seventy-three old?'

'Not really. Not these days. And I promise you I'm not scamming anyone.'

'No? You're sure?'

He was getting annoyed. 'No. I just told you no.'

'The police will have their eye on you now.'

'So what? If they had anything on me, they'd have staked out the place and grabbed me when I came back.'

Meg knew this was true. She didn't want to go on with it either. Not like the endless, pointless disagreements between Nick and his father. They'd follow a pattern. Leon would tolerate his adult son being in the house and pursuing whatever he was pursuing for a while. But then tensions would develop, often over something trivial. Insults would fly, then Nick would shove a few clothes in a shopping bag and leave again. And so it continued until Leon had headaches that became more frequent and severe. He had some difficulty too with hearing and balance, but still insisted to Meg that nothing was wrong. When he finally gave in and had tests, he was diagnosed with an advanced brain tumour. Four months later he was dead.

The year that followed his diagnosis and then his death was the hardest and most painful that Meg had ever experienced. Nick had come home and been warm and supportive, and as the months went by, it became clear that he was back to stay. She overheard him talking one morning to a friend of hers who'd come to say goodbye before moving to Queensland.

'Where are you living?' the friend had asked him. 'And what are you doing with your life?'

'I'm taking it day to day,' he said. 'I'm what you'd call a stay-at-home son.'

Meg recognised it as something of a self-deprecating joke, but at the same time she found it disturbing. A stay-at-home son, she thought. Yes, that's what I've got.

For years it had seemed to her that Nick should be finding a partner, having children, her grandchildren, being a supportive father – all the things that she saw as part of an emotionally rich and worthwhile life. Had she herself had a rich and worthwhile life? She supposed she had, but she'd lately found herself becoming angry with Nick in the way that his father had in the past. She knew that what she was feeling was probably mixed up with her own grief at losing Leon, but even that, like the wake of a ship, turbulent to start with then increasingly calm, seemed to be receding into the past. Her anger with Nick remained.

Small things got to her in a way they hadn't before. Things like him leaving the bathroom in a damp mess or talking endlessly on his phone about something to buy or sell. It also got to her that he'd put a padlock on the door of the back shed. It was Leon's space, and Nick had simply taken it over without asking if she minded. And why a padlock? She wouldn't have done anything with the shed herself, but at the same time, she did mind.

She was also missing the friends that she'd grown up with and had known for most of her life. In the last few years they'd sold up and moved away, mostly to regional towns or to the north or south coast. There was no-one anymore she could meet and talk with over coffee, no-one to help her sort out her feelings about Nick. She'd tried to reason with herself, but it didn't work. She'd turned seventy before she decided to quit her life as a doctor. Some things were beginning to slip. She'd forget a patient's name during a consultation and have to glance at the file on her desk. She'd need to look up the names of medicines she knew well. Then she got a bad case of flu, probably from one of her travelling patients. She recovered but it left her feeling fragile and fatigued. Then she got the flu again in November when it should have been all over. She knew that a doctor wasn't meant to get these illnesses, especially after a vaccine, and she blamed her age.

She gave up her practice six months later and was glad at first that she'd done it. But once the presents and flowers and the thirty-seven bottles of wine had been delivered to her by her patients, and after she'd been told repeatedly how much she'd be missed, there was a new young doctor in her place who was feeling her way into the job, much as Meg had done herself so many years before. She'd begun to see a void ahead of her. She was aware this happened to nearly everyone when they retired, but all the same she knew she'd have to deal with it.

Her anger spilled over one morning while she watched Nick butter his toast and then pile on a crushed avocado.

It had been the only one left in the fridge, and she'd meant to have it herself.

She watched him across the table and a question formed in her mind. It surprised her but she decided to ask it. 'Are you just waiting for me to die?'

Nick frowned. 'What? I don't think so.'

'You haven't thought about it?'

'No.'

'Is that true?'

He smiled at her benevolently – his special warm smile. 'Well, you don't take up much space really.'

There was a pause, and she understood that he was trying to figure out what her question really meant. Nick was good at seeing below the surface.

'What are you really saying?' he asked. 'That you want me to leave?'

'I want you to do more with your life than staying here with me and growing old.'

He took another bite of the avocado on toast. 'The options for my generation are a bit different, Mum, in case you hadn't noticed. I can't easily get a good job and hang onto it. Not the way you and Dad could. So I can't rent anything worth living in. I can't save up and buy a house or even a tiny flat. The prices keep going way out of reach. None of these things are going to happen for most of my generation.'

She knew all this was true but her voice still sounded sharp. 'So you *are* waiting for me to die and then you'll cash in?'

He was clearly disturbed by this and he answered more slowly. 'If you want to put it like that, I suppose so. Unless you leave it all to a homeless dog shelter.'

She got up suddenly and headed for the door. 'I might just do that.' She turned back. 'Oh, and I might sell the house.'

He stared at her. 'What?'

'I need to rationalise things for myself. I need to get rid of the mortgage.'

'And then what?'

'At my age I should find something smaller. Maybe a flat.'

He seemed to recognise that she meant it. 'Where?'

'Somewhere near here. I've lived too long in the Inner West to want to go anywhere else.'

He considered this, then looked at her seriously. 'You won't do it.'

'Won't I?'

She didn't trust herself to say more. Instead she hurried out to the backyard and the screen door banged behind her. She stood breathing in the cool late-winter air that smelled of upturned earth. What was happening to her? It was Leon who'd fought with Nick. She'd told him she was selling the house and he hadn't believed her. She knew he might well be right, and she wouldn't do it, but they did need to talk further about it. But that night she heard the front door gently click shut. It meant he was gone again without telling her when he'd be back.

2

In the morning, and after a troubled sleep, Meg remembered that she had a midday appointment with her lawyer, Jonathan Bell. He'd called to say there were a couple more things relating to Leon's estate that he wanted her to sign in person. He'd explain them to her and then witness them.

Meg had never been entirely comfortable with Jonathan, and she'd thought of finding another lawyer after Leon's death. But time had passed, and she hadn't found the energy for another change, so Jonathan had remained her lawyer. Leon had played golf with him for many years, and she knew that he wouldn't drop a long-term golf partner for anything less than total incompetence.

But it still puzzled her. 'You spend all this time together,' she'd said to Leon once. 'What do you talk about?'

He'd shrugged. 'The game, the weather…'

'What about the wider world, the state of the country?'

'Very rarely and not with Jonathan. But you already know that, don't you?'

Meg did know it. While she and Leon were politically middle-of-the-road or tending to the left, Jonathan was always relentlessly and uncritically conservative. If the conversation ever strayed to politics during the dinners she'd sometimes prepared for Leon's golf partners, Meg usually resisted the temptation to argue, knowing she'd be talked over and patronised by Jonathan and the rest. Sometimes their complacency and bias got too much for her and she would argue back, but Leon would soon give her a warning look. Since she knew that none of their opinions were going to change, she'd give up and bring out the dessert while the conversation settled on golf and other safer topics.

Jonathan's wife, Ella, came to some of these dinners. She was bored by golf, but then she was usually bored by anything that didn't directly concern her. Meg always hoped not to hear more about how rapidly their three sons had risen in their jobs and how they were putting deposits on houses. Ella updated her each time they met, while asking pointed questions about what Nick was doing. But once Leon wasn't there anymore there were no more dinners, and things had changed for Jonathan too. In the past year he'd had a bad case of COVID and then a heart scare. He'd left his position as a high-powered city lawyer and opened a local practice. His new office, up a narrow stairway next to a two-dollar shop, contained only himself and a young female secretary.

As Meg got dressed for her appointment with him, she remembered that Jonathan was particular about clothes. She wondered if she should choose something special, but then settled for the kind of things she usually wore – dark pants, a white shirt and a dark blue jacket. She wondered if she should wear some of her better shoes, but then remembered that the footpaths along the way to Jonathan's office had been made uneven by trees and their roots. No, she'd wear her rubber-soled shoes.

The late winter day was sunny when she set out. There had been rain almost daily in recent months so it was a pleasure to see the sun again. She reached the shopping streets where Jonathan had his new office, and where she and Leon had often eaten together. The shops were colourful and several of them had old-fashioned hand-moulded figures on their awnings. It was a pleasure to see them, and if, as she'd threatened Nick, she sold the house and bought a smaller place, she would still want to be within range of these streets.

She climbed the stairs to Jonathan's office and wasn't surprised to find him on the phone. He was pressing someone for money allegedly owed to one of his clients and was talking in a loud voice about getting a court order. Meg wondered how his secretary, a dark-haired girl in her twenties, coped with hearing him berate people all day.

The girl met Meg with a friendly expression. 'He won't be too long.'

Meg smiled at her. 'Or maybe he will be.'

She laughed. 'True.'

It was more than twenty minutes before Jonathan finally gave up on the call with a parting threat. 'I'll put it in writing and you can expect a visit from my process server.'

He slammed the phone down and came out apologising for the time he'd kept Meg waiting. He glanced at his watch and offered to buy her lunch as compensation. He suggested one of the local Vietnamese restaurants. Meg had expected a short appointment, but she liked the idea of lunch with someone, even if it was only Jonathan. He helped her down the narrow staircase as if she might fall at any moment. The old carpet on the steps was worn, but did he need to be so solicitous – so solicitous for a solicitor? The way he kept touching her back and supporting her arm was almost as if they were on a date rather than going out for a business lunch. But once they were there, Meg felt comfortable the way she always did in Vietnamese restaurants.

She liked how families and other relatives often worked there and how the restaurants seemed to be an extension of their homes. She liked too the mementos on the walls and the smell of cooking. They were sitting near a fish tank with an assortment of well-cared-for fish. Her eyes strayed to them while Jonathan explained the documents in the flat tone of someone who did this too often. Meg knew most of it already, so there was little to understand or talk about. If it had been an office appointment, she'd have left, but she couldn't walk out on a good lunch, most of which had yet to be delivered to their table.

Once the business was done, Jonathan leaned back and looked at her. 'I know Leon went on working almost up to the day he died, but you retired just before the COVID years, didn't you?'

'Yes, though I had no idea of what was coming.'

'It's probably just as well you did. It's been a tough time for GPs.'

'It still is.'

'But you've stayed registered as a doctor, haven't you? And kept your licence to practice?'

'I've not yet used it, but I can if I ever need to.'

He nodded. 'It's part of your identity, I suppose?'

She wondered if he was going to ask her for medical advice. 'I guess it is.'

'Yes…' He drew the word out thoughtfully, then changed the subject. 'I presume you'll want to stay in the house, won't you?'

She could have avoided this question but decided to answer him truthfully. 'I don't know. In fact I'm thinking of selling.'

'Why?' He was clearly surprised. 'I know Leon hasn't left you all that much, but you have your own super too. I'm sure you could manage.'

'I've managed all my life. I'm sick of managing.'

It was true. Although most people would think she'd had a good income as a doctor, it wasn't necessarily so for a GP. There'd been office rental, staff to employ and many other overheads. Specialists made more, but she'd never wanted to specialise. It seemed to her too narrow and you rarely made connections with your patients in the way a GP did.

Jonathan was watching her. 'But that isn't the only reason, is it?'

Meg hadn't planned to tell him about her problems with Nick, but he'd asked a direct question and she found it hard to hold back. She told him that her son was now thirty-one and had lately admitted to his plan to stay at home with her indefinitely. Fuelled by her anger, she explained the police raid and Nick using her computer on the dark web. She was interrupted by the arrival of the main course and she began to regret what she'd said. It wasn't like her, but she couldn't take it back. More people were coming into the restaurant and choosing seats nearby.

Jonathan spoke quietly. 'Tell your son it's not a good idea to be on the dark web.'

'I will, I have. He says he won't use my computer again and I believe him.'

'But he might use his?'

She paused. 'Yes, he might. He says he needs a new one.'

He looked at her for a long moment. 'Do you want to know what I think?'

She hesitated. Did she want to know? But since she'd yelled at Nick over his late breakfast the day before, it felt as if things had changed.

She answered cautiously. 'What?'

'That you should tell him to leave. If he doesn't, then you should put all his things out the front one day when he's out. Then you change the locks.'

It wasn't a surprise to Meg that Jonathan would say this, and also that he would make it sound so simple.

She shook her head. 'I don't see myself doing that.'

Already she regretted telling him anything, but at the same time she did want to hear what he might say.

'It's my view…' He'd said it as if his view would be conclusive. 'That if you raise your children and they get good schooling that leads on to a career, then your responsibility is ended. You don't have to care for them through adulthood, nor should you. You're actually not doing them any favours if you do.'

Meg thought briefly of the way Ella had talked about their sons and how busy they were and how rarely she and Jonathan saw them. She wondered if they too were weary of their parent's fixed opinions and unwanted advice, but she pushed the question aside. She needed to defend her son.

'Nick had reasonably good schooling,' she told Jonathan, 'but it didn't lead to a business of his own, like it did for Leon, or to a career. That happens often enough these days. You get a job and then the company downsizes and the new staff are the first to go. The next job may be worse, night shifts, delivery driver…'

'Or fruit picker and so on, yes, jobs that no-one wants.' He paused and looked at her closely. 'But at the same time, tell me something. Have you heard of elder abuse?'

'What?' She was getting annoyed with him. 'Of course I have, and it's not elder abuse I'm getting from Nick.'

'Are you sure of that? It takes many forms. I'll give you an example.'

She didn't much want to hear it but couldn't see how to stop him.

He went on. 'I had a client, a woman in her sixties. She decided to allow her two adult children to occupy the family home, along with their own kids, while she moved in with a male friend. The relationship quickly broke down and she returned to her own house, where her children and grandchildren were always quarrelling around her. She asked them to leave, but her two children claimed she'd given them the house, although she hadn't. Rather than fight with them, she rented a bedsit and managed on the pension. I advised her to sell the house, but she wouldn't give up the last tenuous connection she had with her children and grandchildren. Then she died.'

Meg took this in. 'So she chose death over kicking out her kids?'

'In part I think she did. At least she faded away very quickly. She may have felt she was solving the problem.'

'And the children kept the house?'

'Oh yes. And fought over it and sued each other. They then had to sell it to pay their legal fees. Neither of them got it in the end.'

They'd finished the meal and the waiter came over to ask about dessert. Jonathan looked at her and she shook her head. She was trying to work out the implications of what he'd just told her.

Her voice was cool. 'Are you saying I should sell the house out from under Nick?'

'It's one solution, if a drastic one. But aren't you already thinking about it?'

This took her by surprise. 'It has…occurred to me, but I love him and we get on well in general. If I sell the house, he might move away. I might lose him altogether. I wouldn't want that.'

Jonathan considered this. 'But if you sold, you could put a deposit on a modest apartment for him in this area.

That would keep him close by, and he'd still be in touch with his friends.'

Meg had sometimes wondered if Nick had real friends because he rarely talked about them. He had several mates that he'd grown up with and a few girlfriends who'd come and gone over the years. Meg had wondered if this was because they could see no viable future with him.

She looked across at Jonathan. 'I could give him the rent on one for a year and then see how things go.'

He shrugged. 'Yes, why not? And you mentioned other reasons for selling, didn't you?'

'Yes, to do with the increasing cost of having a mortgage and other expenses that go with getting older.'

She might have told him more but she could feel his attention shifting. He'd probably had enough of the subject and wanted to get back to the office so he could go on yelling at people over the phone.

She was aware as she said it that it might well be beneath him as a hot-shot lawyer but she asked the question. 'If I did sell, would you be prepared to do the conveyancing?'

He answered slowly. 'Yes, I could...'

'But you don't want to?'

'There are too many idiots in conveyancing these days. You need someone who pays attention and knows what they're doing. You can wind up wasting money on stupidity.'

That, Meg thought, was more like Jonathan. He'd often spoken of the people he dealt with professionally – lawyers, judges, police – in the same dismissive way. As well, he and Ella had a holiday house up the coast and they'd sometimes talked in detail over dinner about the sins of the builders and tradesmen who were all ripping them off.

He went on. 'I'm a little reluctant because it's your home. Yours and Leon's. I miss him, and I walk past it almost every day.'

She answered quietly. 'I miss him too.'

He looked at her. 'I'll do the conveyancing for you if you decide to sell. And if you do, it might work out for the best.'

Jonathan went to the counter to pay the bill, refusing to let her share it. As they left, he held the door open for her and touched her low down on her back, murmuring in her ear, 'I've always fancied you. Did you know that? I always have.'

What could she say to that? She smiled at him uncertainly, and in a moment they were out on the busy footpath. She thanked him for lunch and prepared to walk off in the opposite direction to his office, saying she needed to go to the shops on the way home.

'Keep in touch,' he told her. 'I think you may need some looking after and you know where to find me.' He dropped his voice again. 'And if I may say so, you've still got a nice bum.'

Meg laughed and set off down the busy lunch-time street, passing the shops that had only been her excuse to walk the other way. She was feeling pleased to be told that she had a nice bum at the age of seventy-three, but other elements of their conversation bothered her. She wondered to what degree Jonathan saw her own situation as being much like that of the woman he'd told her about. If he didn't see a parallel, why had he bothered to tell her? But being out in the shopping street reassured her. People nodded to her in passing. A young man said, 'Hello, doctor,' and she smiled back at him and walked on. No, she didn't have two greedy and quarrelling children, and any decision she made about her house would be hers alone.

She reached the front gate and checked her letterbox. In the past she'd always put the glossy ads from estate agents into the recycling bin, but today there was one that was different. It came in the form of a letter on plain brown paper without the photographs or smiling faces. It had her name on it and merely said that if she was thinking of selling at some time in the future, she might consider them as her agents. A man and a woman had signed it. She took the letter with her into the house. She was hoping Nick might already have come back and they could talk. Although he could be annoying and unreliable, he wasn't stupid and there was a good chance they could work something out together. But as she walked into the silent house, she knew he wasn't there.

She went to her bedroom, still carrying the agents' letter, and looked at herself in the long wardrobe mirror. She wondered what there was about her that Jonathan might have fancied once and perhaps still did. She had never been considered a beauty while she was growing up or, she supposed, during her working life, but the parts of her face were in the right place and it was pleasant enough. Leon and others had admired her brown eyes and the light brown hair that waved to her shoulders. Her hair was now almost white and cut short, although some tints of brown remained and were accentuated now and then by her hairdresser. She had lines on her face but not too many.

Once, in her fifties, she'd considered a facelift but Leon had talked her out of it. 'I like you as you are,' he'd said. 'And who else are you doing it for? Some secret lover?' Well, no, she wasn't. And at least her patients seemed to listen to her more closely as she got older. It was as if her aging face gave her a special wisdom. So did that mean she was growing old gracefully and in a way that had attracted Jonathan's approval? As a doctor, she'd never smoked or drunk to excess. She had too often seen up close the damage done to others. She'd also managed to keep her weight down, she walked a good deal and didn't seem to have the aches and pains that many older people, including her friends, regarded as normal. She wondered about her bum and tried to look at it in the mirror. It occurred to her that Jonathan might use it as a standard line. Was he hoping she'd respond? Too bad if he was.

Especially now that Leon was gone, she missed her friends. It seemed as though all of them had recently moved to the country. She'd considered it herself, but if she made that move, how much longer could they all expect to last? Nick wouldn't go with her and he was still, for all his faults, the most important person in her life. She wished he'd been prepared to discuss the matter of the house with her. He might even like the idea of getting his own place out of the deal. She'd tried to call him but his phone was switched off, as it so often was. She suspected that he used another phone for most of his transactions but he hadn't given her that number. As usual, she would have to wait until he turned up.

3

Another day passed and the afternoon sun was low in the sky when she heard an engine loud and close by. The sound stopped and she looked out a front window. Nick was pushing a large black motorbike through the gate. She went out to meet him.

'Whose is that?' she asked wearily, fearing the answer.

'Mine.' He sounded very pleased with himself. 'It's a good one. A Yamaha.'

'Oh yes? And how did you get it?'

'After Pay.'

She'd thought as much. 'So does that mean I'll be paying for it?'

He answered while continuing to admire the motorbike. 'No, I can do it.'

'How?'

'You'll see.'

She knew it would make no difference but she had to say it anyway. 'You know I hate motorbikes. Too many people get killed on them. Statistically, it's a hundred percent certain you'll have at least one accident. There'll always be a driver who doesn't see you.'

'I'll take care.'

How useless was that, she thought? How could you take care when a driver ran a red light or was forced to swerve and failed to see you in the side mirrors? She herself had twice pulled over to the kerb when she'd almost collided with a motorbike rider she hadn't seen. Each time she'd had to stop and calm the beating of her heart before she could drive on. She didn't argue any further with Nick about the motorbike – she knew there was no point – but its noisy arrival had helped her come to a decision.

'I'm selling the house.'

He smiled in a way she found patronising. 'You always say that.'

Had she said it to him more than once? She didn't think so. 'Well, if I have, this time it's for real. I'll pay the rent for you on something for a year, preferably close by and not too expensive. We'll work out what to do for you after that.'

He looked at her. 'I love you, Mum.'

'I'm still selling the house.'

He didn't argue with her but disappeared to his room.

Meg began to walk through the house, thinking about how potential buyers might see it. She went out the back, intending to look in the shed too, but was stopped by a new and solid padlock on the door. She stared at it for a long moment, then went back into the house and called Jonathan. She told him she was taking his advice to sell and would then buy an apartment.

'Is this because of your son?' he asked.

'And my age. Even if I live cautiously, my super and Leon's together might only last till I'm about eighty-five.'

The age of eighty-five had once seemed to her impossibly far off, but now it reared up like a critical barrier.

'You could sell then, or still live in the house on the pension.'

'Yes, I could but…'

He interrupted. 'Well, it's your life. You're choice. Would you like to discuss it over another Vietnamese lunch by any chance?'

No, she thought, *no, no, no.* 'Thank you, Jonathan, but no. There are things I need to get on with now.'

'The place won't take long to sell. We can have lunch together after that.'

She shuddered slightly. 'Yes, that would be very nice.'

Next, she rang the agents who'd sent her the letter. The man and the woman came quickly to see her, both clearly pleased by her response.

'Would you want to go to auction?' the woman asked.

'No!'

Meg didn't want to get caught up in the brutal competition of an auction and she wanted to sell with as few house showings as she could.

The agents arranged cleaners and gardeners, and they began work on the house. Nick came and went on his motorbike, and he seemed untroubled by the extra people. He kept his room tidy but otherwise behaved as if the sale wasn't his concern. Meg was standing in the hall when he came up behind her and poked her in the back.

'It's looking good, Mum. You might want to stay here.'

She knew that he could be right, but she didn't attempt an answer. He went on past her and she saw that he was carrying his motorbike helmet. The front door closed behind him, then she heard its engine. Her resentment welled up, mixed with fear for him, and she admitted to herself that she was only selling the house – or at least selling it now – because of him. He shouldn't live his life this way, and nor should she. Things had to change.

~

The cleaning was done, the cleaners had left and a gardener had replanted the back garden. It was agreed that the house was ready for inspection. Meg was to wait in a nearby coffee bar until the people had walked through and left. She'd been warned that it might take a while, but after the second showing, the agents told her that they had a good offer and advised her to accept it. It meant to Meg that the whole thing would be over quickly, and she said yes. Jonathan handled the paperwork and within a few days the contract was signed. She looked at the scrawled black signatures, including her own. Was that all you had to do to change your life, she wondered? It seemed that it was.

She'd told the two agents that she wanted to buy a flat in the same area, and they'd assured her that there were plenty of good ones. Once she began to look around, there weren't many. Most looked out on nearby buildings with one or two struggling trees or had too much passing traffic noise. Flats were often built on main roads, the agents told her, because the land was cheaper. They'd both shrugged it off as something you just had to put up with if you chose to live in a flat.

The day of settlement was approaching, and Meg had seen almost nothing that she wanted to bid for. Each day she watched the new property ads with growing tension. She knew she could put everything in storage and then continue to look, but she really didn't want that. She felt as if it was all going wrong. Then one evening the man, her own agent, called her to say that something she might like had just come on the market. He had the keys and could show it to her first thing in the morning.

It proved to be in a three-story block of flats on a quiet dead end street. That was good for a start. It was on the ground floor which suited her too. She didn't want to be climbing stairs as she got older. The flat was perhaps smaller than she would have liked, but the setting appealed to her very much. It had a balcony that looked out over a golf course with many trees – Leon's golf course – and beyond was a broad river, the Cooks River. She told the agent he could lock up, that she'd stay outside and think about it. He gave her a contract to read and left her there. She walked down to the river, hearing the wind in the casuarinas along the riverbank. Casuarinas or she-oaks, they went by both names, and on days of any wind she loved the long sighing sound from their multiple grey-green strands. She would have enough for a deposit before her own sale was finalised. Yes, she'd make an offer on the flat.

It was accepted. Jonathan managed the conveyancing and insisted on a check for the manufacture of crystal methamphetamine, the nasty, addictive drug that everyone called 'ice'. The flat had smelled only of air freshener and cleaning fluid to Meg, but the test was done, was negative, and within a few days the contract was signed. The apartment block dated from the sixties and was built of brick, so it was safe from the concrete cancer that plagued more recent buildings. It was a longer walk from the shops but she had her car and she still had Leon's silver-grey Volvo – big, comfortable, twenty years old and very much out of fashion.

After his death, Meg had wondered if she should give up her own car, a blue Toyota Corolla hatchback, and take over Leon's bigger one, but when she'd tried to drive it, the car still smelled too much of him – a mixture of breath mints and Old Spice – and she decided she couldn't handle it. Instead she offered the car to Nick during one of the last breakfasts they would have in the house by the railway line. At least he'd be safer than on the motorbike.

He narrowed his eyes. 'Oh, so you want me to sell the motorbike and use his car instead, do you?'

She knew he'd seen through her. 'Or keep both.'

He shook his head. 'I don't want to be riding around in Dad's car.'

'Why not?'

'It gives the wrong impression.'

'What?' She almost laughed. 'Who to? And why would you care?'

He only shrugged as if it would be too hard to explain to her. 'Why don't you use it? Your car's getting old and you'll have more trouble with it soon.'

'Like what?'

'Like the timing belt going. Wherever you are, the car just stops. It's dangerous if you're in busy traffic.'

'I do know that. And Dimitri keeps an eye on it.'

'Why don't you sell it, not that it's worth much, and keep Dad's?'

She didn't want to spell out to him why she couldn't do that. 'But if you had his car, you could take someone out with you.'

'A girl, you mean? I've got a second helmet.'

She sighed and looked away.

Nick went on. 'If you really don't want his car, I'd get it cleaned up and then sell it for you. I can legitimately say it had one owner who drove it to golf.'

This was only true for Leon's last years, but Meg laughed anyway, then gave up the argument.

'I won't do anything about it yet,' she told him. 'There's space around here to park it. I'll start it up now and then for the battery. You might decide you do want a car.'

Nick shrugged as if he thought it very unlikely but didn't argue. He had already found himself a studio apartment twenty minutes' drive away and closer to the city. It was to be rented in his name and Meg would transfer money to help him. She hadn't seen it and didn't ask much about it. The decisions needed to be his.

On the day she moved into her own flat, Nick was there directing the removalists and helping them to stack the many boxes, which mostly ended up in her bedroom. The empty flat had looked appealing on that first sunny day, but the sky was overcast again and rain showers were forecast for eight days ahead. As well, the place seemed somehow to have shrunk in size. Already she felt let down by that first sunny day.

The removalists left and Meg walked through the place she'd chosen to live in, possibly for the rest of her life. There was a black-carpeted corridor between her flat and the three others on the ground floor. She had the best outlook, but with the space taken up by the new couch and an armchair that had just been delivered, the flat was already beginning to feel overcrowded. The kitchen had looked adequate when she first saw it, but on closer inspection it had little cupboard space and could barely fit a small table and two chairs. There were storage cupboards between the kitchen and bathroom, but they smelled mouldy and so far lacked shelves. If she'd had a garage, she could have put the boxes that were stacked in her bedroom in it, but all she had was a single car space. She'd thought she'd been careful in what she'd chosen to bring, but it was already clear to her that she hadn't been careful enough.

Nick came back into the main room and looked around. 'It'll be tough to fit everything in here.'

'Do you think I don't know that?'

Meg sat down unhappily on the new couch – light cream it had been called when she bought it.

Nick sat in the armchair and looked at the boxes still piled up. 'Well, it's kind of okay… But you don't want to live in a junk yard, do you.'

'Is that what it is?'

'There are ways around it. You could rent a storage space for a fair bit of the stuff.'

Her voice was very flat. 'Then I wouldn't see it or use it, would I?'

He didn't answer.

She went on. 'I'll unpack first and see what's left over.'

'Fair enough.' He was quiet for a moment, then asked her, 'Have you thought about getting a dog?'

'I've made too many decisions lately. I don't want to make any more yet.'

'I've thought of getting one. A rescue dog.' He looked at her. 'You know all the stuff you and Dad thought was wrong with me? Well, maybe it was only because you wouldn't let me have a dog.'

'I've never thought there was anything much wrong with you,' Meg said sharply. 'Nothing that you couldn't deal with if you made up your mind to…'

She cut herself off. She was hearing an echo of something that Leon might have said.

Nick answered with a coolness that had an edge of mockery in it. 'Where there's a will there's a way, you reckon?'

Meg realised that she had effectively lined herself up with Leon in his eyes. 'I'm not saying that.'

'But you're thinking it. I can tell.'

'Don't, Nick. Just don't.'

He got up, kissed her on the cheek, then moved towards the door. 'Goodbye, Mum.'

She felt the pain of this. 'Don't make it sound so final.'

'Well, it is, isn't it?'

Meg was struggling to hold back tears. 'No. I don't know. But it shouldn't be.'

He was already at the door but he looked back and spoke more gently. 'You've earned some peace and quiet, Mum. Make the most of it.'

He left and she heard the motorbike start up. She stayed sitting on the new couch and cried for a long time. The question, 'What have I done? What have I done?' kept echoing in her mind. She had no answer to this, and after a while she went out onto the balcony. As she stood there, she could hear a bass drum being played softly somewhere in the flats. It was a heartbeat sound and was barely audible. The drum seemed to echo inside her and she felt lost and hollow. If she could reverse everything she had lately done, she knew she would. But there was no way back.

Nick stayed away in the week that followed, and Meg tried to convince herself that he was beginning to find his own life and this was his way of proving it to her. By the following week, she couldn't sustain this any longer. She'd made him go out on his own and said something foolish that he'd taken as a reason to stay away. She'd tried to call him, but as usual his phone seemed not to be working and she still didn't have the number of his other phone. She knew the address of his flat and her only option was to turn up at the door, but she didn't want to do that. She'd meant to give him a key to her own flat, but she had only one spare and in the haste and pressure of the move, she'd forgotten to get more cut. She listened for the sound of the bass drum, but it had only continued off and on for a few days after she moved in, then it fell silent.

In the week that followed, Meg spent long hours on the balcony, sometimes reading, sometimes just looking out towards the river and the trees. Now and then there'd be heavy showers, but she rather liked these and the fresh new smells they brought. Once the rain cleared, she listened to the birds settling down and calling to each other at the end of the day. It was pleasant enough but she asked herself if she was really going to spend the rest of her life looking out over green grass, orderly trees and a brown river while being pestered by the sound of golf clubs connecting with balls. She found herself wishing Nick was there to help work out what to do. Almost everything she tried to plan seemed to come back to him. But in the end she'd signed the papers and handed them over, and she knew that she'd done it out of anger, which she also knew was never a good motive for doing anything.

On a mild and cloudy morning, she tried to turn her mind away from the things that troubled her, and set off to walk to the shopping streets. It really wasn't too far and she could get a coffee at a café. There were several ways she could go, and although she knew she probably shouldn't, she chose the one that would take her close to the railway line and past her old house. She could almost hear her father's voice – *when there's nothing you can do, there's nothing you can do*. He was right. She gave up on the idea of walking to a café, and chose a different way back to her flat.

4

Meg was reading on her balcony in the late afternoon when she noticed it was getting unusually dark. There was a rumble of thunder and soon a constant play of lightning in the western sky. When she was thirteen, she'd been walking home from school when lightning struck the powerlines directly above her. She remembered the flash and the ripping sound as if some great force was tearing the air apart. She'd been wary of storms since then.

The lightning was coming closer and she decided to go inside. She was settling herself in the new armchair when she heard a helicopter approaching. The sounds of its engine and whirling blades came closer and closer. Tree branches were cracking, then there was a bang and the light in her flat went out. She had a sudden fear that the helicopter might be about to crash into her building. Should she stay where she was or go outside? Then she heard an immense crunching, dragging sound. It sounded like the helicopter had come down, probably somewhere near the river. She took her medical bag and ran out into the storm.

She could see the helicopter, hunched and dark on the edge of the river. The engine was still running and the smell of wet grass, mixed with aviation fuel, was strong. Behind her, other people had come out of the flats but had remained at a safe distance. She saw only one man close to the crash site and could hear his voice distantly as he talked on his phone. She ran on, and she could see that the body of the helicopter was more or less intact and so were the doors and windows. There were two people inside – the pilot and his one passenger, who looked like a young boy – and neither were moving, held in place by their seatbelts. Meg started towards the nearest door, which was on the passenger side and away from the river. The man who'd been talking to triple zero shouted something at her, but she couldn't hear him because of the engine noise and the continued rumbling of the storm. She ran on towards the nearer door.

Hands grabbed her hard from behind and she heard a male voice. 'Get back, you stupid woman!'

She tried to shake him off. 'I can get to them through that door. I'm a doctor.'

'You'll be an ex-doctor if you try that.'

Then she saw it herself. One of the rotor blades must have been damaged in the crash. It was still turning and was dipping low, almost touching the grass as it turned. Meg recognised what would have happened to her if she'd gone to that door. The man could see she understood it now and released his grip.

She found it difficult to speak. 'What are we going to do?'

'We can't do anything till the engine's shut down. I'm going to see if I can get to the door on the other side.'

'Then what?'

He picked up a golf club near his feet. 'If it won't open, I'll try to break the window. But keep back. The fuel tank's ruptured. There's Avgas everywhere.'

She watched as he slid down the steep slope to the river, then circled back towards the pilot's door. When he was close enough, he stopped, watching the blades turn. He seemed to be counting the number of seconds he might have, and then, as the damaged rotor blade passed, he dived into a space by the pilot's door and crouched there. The rotor blade continued to sweep by and Meg could see that it was missing the back of his head by only a few centimetres.

He tried the door but it was jammed shut. He stood carefully and swung the golf club at the window, avoiding the lethal rotor blade as it swooped by. Meg watched as the golf club bounced off the window several times, but then the glass finally broke. He smashed more of it so he could get through. He disappeared inside and there was a pause. Then she heard the engine cut out and the rotor blades slowed and came to a stop.

He reappeared and called to her. 'You can try the other door now.'

She reached it but it was still stuck.

The man had already got it open on the river side. 'Come round this way.'

As he helped her to the open door, she noticed several bleeding cuts on his hands from the broken window. She went first to the pilot, who was unconscious. Meg checked his breathing and was relieved to find it more or less steady.

The boy looked very shaken but at least he was awake. She guessed his age to be about fourteen and noticed that he was wearing a short-sleeved shirt, a tie and shiny new shoes. She scrambled over to him and managed to open the other door from the inside.

'Can you get us out now?' he whispered.

'I don't want to move you. There are ambulances on the way.' As she said it, she heard the sirens approaching. 'They're nearly here.'

The boy was close to panic. 'But it might catch fire!'

'Not now. We've turned off the engine.'

He was beginning to cry. 'My neck hurts.'

'The paramedics will brace it and get you out.'

'Will you stay with me?'

'Yes, I will.'

But then she felt the helicopter slide a little further towards the river. She waited and it seemed to steady. Then it slipped a little more.

'I'm going to take your seatbelt off,' she told the boy.

If the helicopter went into the river, she might at least save him. She put her arm around him while she took the seatbelt off. He flopped forward and cried out in pain. She held him, bracing him as well as she could.

'My uncle does traffic reports,' he managed to say. 'But the storm came up from nowhere. I was doing…work experience. He said we mightn't make it all the way back, but we could land on the golf course… Why doesn't he wake up?'

She knew the pilot could have landed safely if he hadn't hit the trees and then the powerlines, but she answered only, 'The ambulances are nearly here for you both.'

Less than a minute later two paramedics came to the open door. Meg told them she was a GP and she thought the boy probably had compression injuries. She said the pilot was breathing but still unconscious. She murmured quietly, hoping the boy wouldn't hear, that the helicopter had been slipping and there was a risk of it going into the river. They helped her get out carefully and took over. Police and firemen were arriving too.

She noticed the man who'd saved her from the broken rotor blade and went over to him. They stood without speaking while the boy's neck was braced and he was taken on a trolly to one of the ambulances. The helicopter slipped once more, but the pilot was safely out by then and on a stretcher. The ambulances drove away and the sirens faded. She asked the man to show her the cuts on his hands. She could see that the bleeding had more or less stopped, but she checked the cuts for any remaining glass, then put antiseptic and light bandages on each hand.

She was repacking her medical bag when she heard him say, 'I'm sorry I called you a stupid woman.'

She spoke over her shoulder as she worked on. 'Because a man would have handled it better?'

'Not at all. I could've called you a stupid man just as easily.'

She turned to look at him, then found herself staring. Something about him seemed very familiar.

'Don't I know you?' she asked.

He seemed to be deciding whether or not to respond or simply walk away. He came to an uneasy decision. 'Yes, I think you do.'

'…Colin?'

His name alone brought with it a rush of confusion, old hurts and buried regret.

He turned away from the broken helicopter. 'Let's go.'

They walked in silence across the wet grass, and Meg was glad that she didn't have to say anything more just yet. Nearer to the flats, people were still watching the efforts by the firemen and others to stabilise the helicopter. A television news van was arriving.

A woman from the flats came up to them with her little boy. She was in her mid twenties and had a gentle Asian face. Meg knew that she had one of the ground-floor flats near her.

'Those two people in the helicopter, the man and the boy, do you think they'll be all right?' she asked.

Meg hesitated. 'Yes, I do.'

'That's a relief.' She turned to the little boy. 'We'll go home now.'

He looked as though he didn't want to leave, but his mother gripped his hand firmly and they set off. Meg wished they'd stayed. She felt strangely exposed standing beside Colin again after the five decades that had passed. It was as if the choices she had made, and the mistakes, were suddenly laid open to a stranger. Except he wasn't a stranger. He was a man she'd known many years ago, a man she had loved and believed she had lost.

He seemed taller than she remembered, or maybe it was she who'd shrunk with age. His hair was grey and thinning, and he seemed fit enough at first glance, but she noticed a slight forward stoop. His eyes were dark brown and observant, as they had always been, and his face was lined. Of course it would be, she thought. Of course it was. She even remembered his age and when he was born. January 8, 1946, a critical birth date. She was seven months younger.

'What were you doing here?' she asked. She hadn't meant it to be an accusing question, but she knew it sounded like one.

'I heard the crash.'

'Does that mean you play golf here or...?'

She was thinking of the golf club he'd used to get into the helicopter and turn off the engine.

'No. I nabbed the club from a golf buggy. I put it back.'

'But why were you here?'

He looked at her with an expression that was hard to read. 'I live here.'

'Where?' She'd said it as if it was something that wasn't possible.

'In that street up there.' He pointed to a street that came over the crest of the hill above the golf course and then stopped in a turning circle. 'You go over the ridge and then I'm a few houses down on the left.'

'What number?'

'Forty-two.'

She shook her head. She had no reason to doubt this but it was still hard for her to absorb.

'I live here too now.' She pointed to the flats. 'I moved here from a house by the station three weeks ago.'

He only nodded as if he already knew where the house was. She had no idea what to say next, but he continued. 'It's not that strange, you know. Birds come back to where they were hatched.'

'Or maybe they never left. Like me.'

There was a pause, and then he asked as if uncertain, 'Would you…' He stopped.

'Would I what?'

'Like a drink?'

She noticed that several local people were pointing them out to the news crew. She was still feeling shaken by what had happened and wanted to get away.

'Yes, I'd like a drink. But where?'

'The golf club perhaps?'

She looked at the path that followed the river as far as the golf club. Night was beginning to fall and the path wasn't paved. It would be wet and slippery after the storm. She thought of inviting him back to her flat instead, but the windows were still dark and her torches and candles were somewhere in one of the still unpacked boxes in her bedroom.

'I don't know if they'll be serving food because of the blackout, but they may well have drinks,' he was saying. 'We could walk down and see. Are you cold though?'

She was cold. 'No.'

They turned to leave, then she saw the members of the news crew hurrying towards them – a reporter, a cameraman, a soundman and an assistant carrying lights.

Colin turned away and his voice had a harsh edge. 'I don't want to talk to them. Let's go.'

Meg didn't want to talk to them either. What could you say about the crashed helicopter and the two people in it? You could only repeat the usual cliches that followed such an accident. She and Colin walked quickly towards the head of the path, but the news crew increased their pace and caught up with them.

The young male reporter approached Meg first, the assistant swung the light onto her face and the cameraman and soundman took up positions. She noticed that Colin was quietly retreating in the background towards the riverbank. Did he hope the dark trees might hide him from these people?

'You're the doctor who was first on the scene?' the reporter was saying to her.

Meg shifted her medical bag to her shoulder, noticing that it seemed unusually light. Could she have dropped some things by the helicopter? No, it was still zipped up.

'Yes, I live close by. I'm a GP, a retired GP.'

'Can you tell me anything about the condition of the people on board?'

'No, I can't. I could only check on them and try to stabilise things as best I could. You'll need to talk to the police or the hospital for anything more.'

'You can't tell us how bad you think their injuries were?'

'No, I can't.'

She was already annoyed with the reporter. He'd know that families must be notified first so why did he bother to ask? The assistant nudged him and pointed to Colin, a dark figure standing still among the trees. The crew charged towards him and the lights were shone full in his face.

The reporter began. 'You're Peter Brown, we're told, a local resident...'

Meg was puzzled. That wasn't his name. Colin said nothing but stared blank-faced at the reporter as he went on.

'We're told you got into the helicopter and turned off the engine when it was about to catch fire. And then it was sliding into the river with the pilot and his young passenger still on board. Isn't that right?' He paused for a moment, but Colin didn't respond.

The reporter continued, 'How did you feel when you heard the crash? Did you actually see it or just hear it?'

Colin put up his hand to stop the questions. 'Listen, I don't want to be interviewed. I don't give you permission to use this footage either.'

'We can always blur your face if you want us to.'

Meg noticed that the red light on the camera was still on.

'No. I want you to scrap it.'

The reporter shrugged. 'Okay, it's your call. It's a pity though.'

Who was it a pity for, Meg wondered? The reporter nodded to the cameraman, who stopped filming. He turned back to Meg. 'You don't have a problem, do you, Mrs…um? I mean with having your face on TV?'

She answered reluctantly. 'No.'

'So can we ask you a few more questions?'

She could see Colin's grim expression. It was clear that he wanted to get away and might even walk off without her.

'No,' she told the reporter flatly. 'There's nothing more I can tell you.'

The soundman pointed to something happening over by the helicopter and they moved away.

'Can we go now?' Colin asked her, his voice hard and impatient.

He had a small torch on his key chain and used it to guide them along the muddy path that followed the river to the golf club. The clouds were clearing and there was some light from the rising three-quarter moon. It was a relief to Meg to be away from the nauseating smell of aviation fluid, now replaced by the familiar smells of the river and the mangroves. But she still felt shaken by what had just happened. She also found it hard to recognise much in the man walking beside her. What she had loved about him from the age of fifteen was his calm and his depth of understanding. He wasn't like most of the young men she had known at the time. She'd seen some similar qualities in Leon, which wasn't surprising because he was Colin's best mate in those years. She had always liked Leon too back then, but Colin had been the one for her.

As she walked carefully down the dark path with him, she wondered how it might have been for them both if the ball with his birthdate on it had not been picked out of the barrel or if Leon, who'd been born in the same year, had been the one conscripted instead. She felt guilty at once about even having such thoughts. It was unfair. She had come to love Leon and would not have wished anything like the Vietnam war on him or anyone else, but at the same time she knew that it would have been different. If Colin had escaped the Birthday Ballot, it was likely that, in their twenties, they would have married and had one or more children and a different life.

Colin was still using his little torch to guide them along the uneven path, keeping his hand lightly on Meg's elbow in case she slipped. 'I was at home and I could hear the chopper was in trouble,' he told her. 'The sound of the engine was wrong, then it began to falter.'

'Do you fly helicopters? Or did you…over there?'

'No, I was a conscript, a nasho, and they didn't let us fly helicopters, but we travelled in them.'

Meg tripped momentarily on a tree root and he gripped her elbow to steady her. The river shone dark and smooth, disturbed only when a fish broke the surface.

She needed to ask the next question. 'Is there someone…?' She stopped.

'You mean is there someone at home just over the ridge? No. Not anymore. I did have a wife but she left me eight years ago. She married again so we're not really in touch.'

'Do you have…'

'Children? Yes, one. Elizabeth. Beth we call her.'

'Where is she now?'

'Living in the Blue Mountains, but she catches the train to the Western University campus in Parramatta. She's close to getting her degree.'

Meg noticed that he had mentioned his daughter's name but not his wife's.

There was another question she needed to ask. 'And you know Leon died, do you?' There was no way to say it tactfully.

'Yes, I do.'

They walked on in silence. Leon's death wasn't something she could talk about on an unlit muddy path with a likelihood of falling. But she had one more question. 'Why didn't you want them to film you?'

He sighed. 'Can we let that one go for now?'

She wanted to ask more. The incident with the news crew still felt uncomfortable, and what did she really know about the man she was walking away from the crash site with in the dark?

He seemed to understand this and spoke as if with difficulty. 'It goes back a long way. To Vietnam.'

'And you're Peter Brown now?'

'I am, legally. And that name's given me peace for a few years.'

'And you don't want to tell me why?'

'No, I don't. Not now. Not yet.'

She liked the way 'not yet' implied some future contact between them. 'So what should I call you?'

'Colin. Same as always.'

She took this in. 'And did you just save my life?'

'Probably.'

'Then thank you…Colin.'

They looked at each other in the semi-dark, then walked on.

5

Lights were flickering in the darkness and music was playing softly as they climbed the steps to the golf club. It was a building modest in size and furnished without unnecessary expense. It wasn't full of poker machines either, like so many of the bigger clubs. Meg had come here a few times with Leon but, with the electricity shut down, the candles and the lamplight meant that the place appealed to her in a way it never had before.

Colin glanced at Meg. 'You okay with this?'

'Yes, it's good.'

There were people at the tables but the conversations were unusually quiet. Golfers often talked loudly after a game, like returning warriors who wanted to tell everyone within earshot what they'd achieved out on the course. Most of the people there that night seemed to be locals shaken by what they'd just witnessed. They all knew that it could have been worse, a change in the wind might have caused the helicopter to crash into the nearby flats and houses.

'The pilot did well to put it down,' a middle-aged man was saying as they passed his table. 'Pity that he clipped the trees and the powerlines, but he still controlled it as well as he could.'

Colin chose a table in the far corner with a lighted candle on it and left Meg there while he went to the bar. As she waited, she could feel that her heart was beating fast, and she began to think this drink might not be such a good idea. Should she simply get up and leave? Colin was clearly uncertain about her and would let her go without protest. But, no, she shouldn't leave. He'd been too significant in her early life for her to walk out on him now. 'Don't I know you?' she had asked him. Oh, yes, she did.

She continued to watch him as he waited patiently at the bar, not protesting when a woman pushed in ahead of him but stepping aside for her. It was as if she was seeing more of the boy and young man he used to be, and now it was Colin who was still alive while Leon, who'd escaped the war, was dead. The three of them had become friends in high school and she was soon known as Colin's girlfriend. Up through the ages of fourteen and fifteen, she and Colin fumbled together but pulled back. She turned sixteen and still they waited. Then school was over and it was the day of her seventeenth birthday.

They had gone out that morning for an impromptu birthday celebration in the city and it was decided, with a little hesitancy, what they would do that day. Meg waited outside a pharmacy while Colin bought condoms, then they went looking for a hotel. There wasn't much alternative. They both lived at home, neither of them had a car and hiding in the bushes along a local path or near the railway line wasn't much of an option. Waiting for it to get dark wouldn't help either. There was a birthday dinner with her family planned for Meg that evening and she couldn't be late for that.

She waited outside each hotel while Colin went in to ask for a room. At each hotel, the reception staff took one look at an underdressed seventeen-year-old with no luggage and told him the hotel was full. It was the middle of the day and it meant a long and tiring walk from the centre of the city towards Central Station where there might be cheaper and less fussy hotels.

They were nearing the station and feeling as if they'd walked miles when they reached the People's Palace, the Salvation Army hotel. Colin had seemed bothered by the religious element in the name.

'Should we be doing it here?' he'd asked her.

She felt they had walked too far to back out. 'Maybe not but let's try. I'll come in with you and we can say we're Mr and Mrs. I can keep my left hand in my pocket so they can't see if I've got a ring.' She'd hesitated, then decided to ask something more that had been troubling her. 'Do you know how to do it? I mean if we get in?'

'I think we'll figure it out.'

The man at the desk looked at them dubiously but didn't argue and gave them a cheap room on the top floor. The metallic folding mesh of the lift door clashed behind them, then the lift travelled upwards very slowly. Meg remembered a woman of about sixty who'd been already in the lift as it came up from the basement. She'd stared accusingly at them both during the slow ascent as if she knew what they intended to do and was trying to shame them into giving up and going home to their families instead.

Meg remembered the double bed that took up most of the tiny room and squeaked loudly as if to deter any movement. It was painful for her to start with, but Colin was careful and restrained, and in the end it felt right and even nice and a lot less mysterious. She remembered lying back in the bed and watching the pigeons on the window sill. A male was following several females about, bobbing his head and cooing at them in a soothing way as if he hoped to persuade them to remain still long enough for him to mate with them.

On the train back to the Inner West with Colin beside her, Meg found herself looking out the window and smiling with guilty pleasure.

A young boy sitting opposite had leaned over. 'Is it your birthday? You look happy.'

She'd laughed. 'Well, yes, it is.'

Colin had smiled at her too and moved closer. He had to be home to look after his younger brother while their parents were out, but he walked her home and left her at the gate while she went in to have her birthday dinner. What would he still remember of it all, she wondered? Nothing much perhaps. He had asked her to have a drink with him, a drink that was taking a while to buy, and she was feeling both strangely pleased but also uneasy.

There was too much hurt in their past. Why let it come back to life in a present in which she had, mistakenly, put her house up for sale and evicted her stay-at-home son?

She should be looking for some peace and steadiness in her life. She needed to join a book club and meet other people. I don't need my first love just now, she thought. I don't want to be told I'm to blame for what happened in his life. I don't need this. She pushed her chair back, reached for her medical bag, and stood up. But then she saw that he was already on his way back to the table.

He came up to her as she stood frozen with her medical bag. 'Were you going to the toilet?'

'Ah…no.'

She sat down and so did he.

'You were leaving?' He'd asked this as if he was not much surprised.

'I…thought of it.'

'Go ahead if you want to. It's up to you. Just be careful on the walk back. You'd better take my torch.'

'And you can see in the dark?'

He didn't answer immediately and she realised that he too was very tense. Somehow it eased her own tension while at the same time the candle on their table made her feel enclosed with him. It was as if they could speak more directly to each other without the room's overhead lights on. People at other tables also seemed to be leaning forward in the candlelight and speaking more softly and intimately than usual.

He responded to her question. 'I can see well enough. There's no reason for you to return the torch.'

'But you're a neighbour now so perhaps I could come over with it. What do you think?'

He leaned back and looked at her in the candlelight. 'I think I would like that.'

'But you're not sure?'

He sat back and she saw the sudden anger in his expression, so strong that it frightened her. 'How can I be sure, given the way you left me.'

Meg felt she couldn't let it go at that. 'Or the way you left *me*. I would have tried, you know.'

'Except you didn't try very hard.'

'You were back from Vietnam and full of...' She hesitated. 'Fury.'

'And grief.'

'Yes, and grief. It was a bad war.'

'It was. And all of us who fought there were somehow to blame for it, including conscripts like me. We didn't deserve that.'

'I didn't blame you.'

He leaned towards her. 'Then why did you ask me first thing if I'd killed anyone?'

She looked down. 'I'm not sure. I guess I wanted to know.'

'And of course I had. They were trying to kill me. Or at least I thought I had. Killed someone, I mean. So much of the time we'd fire at noises in the dark but not actually know if we'd hit anyone.'

There was a pause.

Meg wasn't sure what the effect on him would be, but she had to say it. 'I'm sorry about that night. I was young and stupid.'

'And to top it off you'd fallen for Leon, my best mate.'

'I hadn't fallen for him then.'

'But you were sleeping together.'

'I didn't know if you were ever coming back. You didn't answer my letters.'

He shook his head. 'Perhaps because I didn't get them. The commanders didn't want us to know too much about the marches and protests going on here. They held the letters back for months at a time.'

'I didn't know that.'

'No. You didn't. I didn't either. I didn't know why you hadn't written.'

She could imagine something of how that would have been. 'And then you got all my letters at once, I suppose.'

'Eventually, yes, though there weren't many of them. And when I did get them, was I supposed to be pleased that you and Leon were demonstrating against the war?'

'Leon only came to the demonstrations because I wanted him to. He wasn't all that committed.'

'Makes sense. But you were committed.'

'Yes, I was.'

They said nothing for a little while. The door opened for people leaving and the draft made the candle flicker. As more people left, the opening and shutting of the door caused a draft each time, but the flame didn't go out.

She finished her wine and Colin asked her if she'd like another. She hadn't realised she was drinking so fast but, yes, she would. She'd have offered to buy it but she had only her medical bag with her, no money, and a card wouldn't work in the blackout. Colin set off for the bar and she was glad to be on her own for a little while. She looked around the room. Tables had been emptying and there were fewer people at the bar so he was already getting served. She realised she was very cold and rubbed her arms. Colin must have noticed because, when he came back with the drinks, he took off his jacket.

'I don't need it.' He put it around her shoulders. 'I have a sweater on as well.' He sat down. 'So here we are. Two lonely people coming to the end of our lives.'

It irritated Meg to be called lonely even though it was true. She found the way he'd said it depressing as well.

He noticed her reaction. 'Or maybe you're not lonely.'

'Are you?'

'I have enough to do. What about you?'

He was looking at her closely and it was clear that he wanted a truthful answer.

She attempted one. 'I'm having trouble refocusing since I sold my house and moved here. It was in part so my son would have to move out and, I hoped, find a life of his own. He calls himself my stay-at-home son.'

'How old is he?'

'Thirty-one.'

'So really stay-at-home.'

'Not anymore. I'm in a one-bedroom flat and he's in a rented studio apartment a couple of suburbs away. And, yes, I'm a bit lonely too but I'm working on it. I've got a list of book clubs.'

He looked amused. 'Good, but there are alternatives to book clubs, you know.'

She didn't ask what they were. They raised their glasses to each other and this time she drank more slowly, aware that she had to make it back along the slippery path. They watched the candles on the tables around them flickering out one by one. Colin seemed to be wondering whether or not to say something.

When he finally spoke, his voice was harsh. 'You know when you were deciding for Leon instead of me…'

Meg started to say it wasn't like that.

He ignored her interruption and went on. 'You should have sent me a Dear John letter.'

She was both startled and puzzled by this. She couldn't have sent a Dear John letter because she'd never thought of breaking up with him. As long as he lived through his two years of training and service, she knew the time would come when he could leave the army and return home. She'd been anxious for his safety every day. She'd often lain awake at night unable to sleep because of her growing fear for him as the casualty reports came in. She'd never taken the encounters with Leon too seriously. It was troubled times and they'd just happened. It meant there might be something to deal with when Colin came back or there might be nothing at all. She registered what he was saying.

'It would have been better for you to write to me and tell me while I had mates around me who'd have helped me let go. I needed to know and not to walk into it on my first day back.'

Meg had to protest. 'But I wasn't deciding anything. I was waiting until you came home. I knew I wouldn't know anything for sure till I saw you again.' She repeated it. 'I was *waiting* for you.'

'Would you have told me about Leon?'

'I might have. It was the sixties after all.'

'So you wanted a threesome?'

'No!' The question had startled her. She couldn't say anything for a moment but then she shook her head. 'No, it wasn't like that.'

'Like what?'

'Just sex. It wasn't like that. I…loved you both.'

'Yes, well, I'd thought I was coming home to a safe place and there were you and my best mate together. The worst grenade of all.'

Meg could find nothing to say to this. She noticed that the golf club had emptied further. It would close soon.

'Where did you go then?' she asked.

'Back to the army for a while. I said I wouldn't go back to Vietnam so they found me a job in Darwin looking after army stores and weapons. Very boring in its way but also welcome. Then a few years passed and I left the army and there were jobs for ex-soldiers.'

'In Darwin?'

'And elsewhere.'

'You could've gone to university.'

'Back here? Along with you and Leon? No thanks.'

'I was only an ex-girlfriend. Most men collect a few ex-girlfriends along the way. It shouldn't have affected your whole life, or what you did with it.'

'It was you and Leon and Vietnam in combination. My best mate and the girl I was going to marry when I got back. And then there was too much I'd seen in Vietnam. Too much that had happened.'

'Do you…?'

He seemed to shudder slightly. 'Want to talk about it? About Vietnam? No, I don't.'

'I wasn't going to say that.'

He sounded sceptical. 'What were you going to say?'

'I was going to ask if you had, or are still having, any kind of treatment for it all? For PTSD?'

'You mean psychotherapy? Yeah, hours and hours of it. It eased things for a while. I thought less of suicide.'

'But do you…?' She hesitated.

'Do I what? Think about it still? Well, look at the numbers. The men who've killed themselves since the war. That should tell you something.'

The implication that she'd been too dumb or inattentive to notice veteran suicides got to her. 'I had a patient. Her husband had been in Vietnam. He was thirty-two when he killed himself leaving her with three small children.'

'And you helped her, I suppose.'

She could still hear the anger in his voice but she tried not to react to it.

'I did what I could. She made it through and the kids grew up and were okay as far as I know. I treated quite a few people that the war had…affected.'

'Atoning, were you?'

'What?'

'Atoning for Leon?'

It was an odd and difficult question but she knew what he meant. 'Maybe…Yes, I guess I was, in part anyway.'

'If it had been anyone else, I think I could've managed, might even have accepted it, but I'd lost my best mate as well. That was too much.'

She couldn't think of anything to say. She knew that in a real sense he was right. Decisions had been made almost without recognising them and on a step-by-step basis, until she and Leon had been to an anti-war rally and ended up making love in his dad's car where, in some way, it seemed such an insignificant thing in comparison to everything else that was happening. She knew it would make no difference but she said it anyway. 'It wasn't really a decision. It just happened.'

'Like so many things.' He seemed to be making up his mind whether or not to go on with the argument. Then he said abruptly, 'I cheated on you too though, you know.'

She let this sink in, wondering what he meant by admitting to it now. She answered mildly. 'I guess it was hard not to.'

'It was. I was a rifleman and we'd go out on patrol knowing that at any time we could walk into an ambush or step on a landmine. You can see so little when you're forcing your way through jungle, knowing your life depends on the man ahead of you and the man behind you. It was only their eyes and their instincts that kept you alive, plus some dumb luck.'

'And I suppose you were desperate for distraction.'

'Yes.' His shoulders dropped. 'And then when I was rushed back here by plane, and when we met that night, of course I didn't know how to tell you. So many Vietnamese girls only started things with soldiers because they thought it might help their families. And many families didn't make it through the war. But I had seen her a few times, and I almost felt as if I was falling in love with her. Then suddenly they told me I was flying back to Sydney the next day. I didn't know what I was going to tell you… Then I saw you and Leon.'

'I didn't mean for it to happen that way.'

'No? You would have lied to me, would you? Kept it from me?'

It was hard for her to answer truthfully. After all this time she didn't remember what her intentions might have been or even if she'd had any. 'Maybe. I don't know.'

He paused and shifted in his seat, then sighed. The memory was difficult. 'And it wasn't much that I saw. It was only you two walking together in the street. You weren't even touching each other. But he said something and you looked round at him and I knew.'

Meg let this sink in, then she asked, 'Did you hate me very much?'

'I was twenty-two and the army had taught me how to hate. They specialise in that, you know.'

'And you've hated us both all these years?'

'I'd hear news of what you were doing. When you got married, the baby and then, later on, when Leon died.'

'You didn't come to his funeral.'

They were both silent again as if there was either nothing left to say or too much to say.

Colin stirred first. 'I'll walk you home.'

'You won't drown me in the river on the way?' she asked lightly.

'I'm still deciding.'

She didn't in fact fear that he would, but a sense of an underlying threat still gripped her. She knew that maybe she should leave it alone at this point, but there was something more she needed to ask. 'Do you still hate him? Do you still hate me?'

'What's the point? But if it tells you anything, I hadn't gone looking for you.'

'And you hadn't planned on saving my life?'

'I'll walk you back.'

He'd said it in a tone that meant she shouldn't argue and as if he thought there might still be some danger out there.

'So you can save me from more crashing helicopters?'

'If necessary.'

He stood up, looking tall and strong and purposeful, ready to walk into the night. She looked up at him for a long moment, then she stood up too.

6

Although the three-quarter moon was higher now and giving some light, the path along the riverbank was still wet and dark because of overhanging trees. Colin kept his torch on the path in front of them while again keeping a light but reassuring touch on Meg's elbow in case she slipped. She was glad that she didn't have to walk back alone. Two nightbirds screeched to each other as they followed the winding river towards the sea, and the light of another small torch came bouncing towards them. Meg saw that it belonged to a woman walking a big dog. She couldn't see it clearly but the black and brown suggested that it was a rottweiler. She drew closer to Colin as the woman and the dog approached.

He glanced at her. 'I remember that you don't like dogs. It was because one went for you as a kid, wasn't it?'

'It's only the big ones I don't much like. The smaller ones are fine.'

The woman nodded to them as she and the dog passed by. Meg looked after them thinking that a woman could safely walk anywhere at night with a big dog, even along a dark riverbank.

Colin had noticed her expression. 'Do you want a dog?'

She hesitated. 'I don't think so. Getting approval from the other residents could be hard. At my age, I don't need a dog to look after all the time. Or a son.'

'Is that why you moved here?'

'More or less. I thought at my age I should free myself from the house and garden. And, yes, I also wanted some freedom from my only son, Nick, Nicholas. My beloved son, I should add.'

'And were you right or wrong?'

'Wrong, I think. Almost certainly wrong.' Something was puzzling her still. 'Why did you come back here? To this suburb? To the street where you are now?'

'Didn't I tell you that? It was because I'm like a bird. I'm programmed to come back to a place I know, a place where I grew up and then left. Though leaving wasn't my idea.'

In a silence that followed, Meg could hear the night sounds in the trees and along the river. A fish jumped and she saw the tiny waves it stirred up as they rippled in the moonlight, then settled back.

Colin corrected himself. 'Or perhaps I'm more like a mullet. They always come back here too.'

A further thought came to Meg. She couldn't see much sense in what she was about to ask him but she said it anyway. 'So is there anything I could do to make up for it all? Or at least a bit?'

Colin turned to look at her. 'What?'

'You heard me.'

'You want to make up for, what is it? Fifty years?'

'Yes. For my part in it. I don't take responsibility for the war. Or the Birthday Ballot.'

'Don't you? Are you sure you didn't organise that too?'

She merely looked at him and they walked on but it was clear that he was musing on what she'd said.

After a few more minutes he asked, 'So what are you offering me then? A fuck?'

She responded with a startled laugh. 'No. At least I don't think so.'

'But it's not out of the question?'

'Where have I heard that before?'

He looked at her narrowly. 'It was one of Leon's lines. He said it sometimes worked.'

She knew he was waiting to see if she'd react badly to this. She decided not to, though her voice was cool. 'I guess that could be Leon. And maybe you knew him better than I did.'

'In some things perhaps. I know that he loved you.'

She glanced at him.

'Yes, he did,' Colin went on. 'Even back when we were all nineteen. And I knew he was jealous of me because I had you and he didn't.'

She had nothing to say to that. The water lapped as a small boat passed on the river.

'How did you feel when your number was drawn out of the barrel and his wasn't?'

He deflected the question. 'It was a real barrel, you know. Made of polished blackwood. It used to be owned by Tattersall's Lottery.'

She looked at him steadily in the dark, waiting for a real answer.

It came slowly. 'I thought that if one of us had to go, it'd better be me. I'd cope better. I thought Leon wouldn't have handled the training. It was quite brutal, you know.'

'I know.'

'Then I thought he'd probably step on the first landmine that he came across.'

'I guess he might have. But you avoided them all?'

'I didn't lose any limbs but I was nearby. Very nearby. I've got the scars, the shrapnel wounds, and I'm a bit deaf in one ear too. My left ear.'

'So someone else stepped on a mine?'

'More than one.'

They walked on in silence and soon there were more bright lights ahead in the open area where the helicopter had crashed. A large machine was pulling it away from the river and towards more level ground and the broken rotor blade was dragging through the grass. Seeing it like this confirmed again for Meg that if Colin hadn't grabbed her back, it would have killed her. But how, she wondered, do you go on adequately thanking someone for saving your life, someone who probably hates you? He was looking at her sidelong and she realised that he understood what she was thinking and that she didn't need to say any more.

Instead she asked, 'Do you know how they'll do it from here?'

'They'll take off the blades, then the body of it will be put on a truck.'

'A big truck.'

'Well, yes, and the rotor blades will need to travel separately, but as helicopters go, it's not that big. You don't need a big one when you're only reporting on traffic jams.'

She thought about the boy in the front seat and also about the pilot. She'd judged the pilot to be in his thirties, with much of his life ahead of him. While they stood watching, the streetlights came back on, and so did the lights in the flats, including hers. She was glad of it – she'd had enough of the dark. They watched the recovery of the helicopter for a little longer, then Colin escorted her to her flat.

When they reached the door, Meg got out her key and looked around at Colin. He seemed to be making up his mind.

'What is it?' she asked.

'I was wondering if I should kiss you goodnight.'

'I thought you don't like me?'

'Maybe it's because…' He stopped.

'We go a long way back?'

'Not only that.'

They had talked a lot that night, but she could see that there were things still unsaid. He might tell her what they were, she supposed, or he might not.

She unlocked the door. 'Then let's delay the decision. If you come in, we can watch the late news for a report on the crash.'

He followed her into the main room of the flat and she noted the way his size made it feel smaller. She hadn't unpacked many of her things yet, like her pictures or carved figures, and she knew the place appeared bare.

Colin was looking around. 'You have a white couch,' he remarked, sounding a little surprised.

'They called it light cream when I bought it. My dark blue couch was too big to fit here. I thought a light-coloured one might make the place feel bigger.' She looked at it doubtfully. 'Probably another mistake.'

'Another?'

'I've made plenty of them.'

She turned on the TV and they sat together on the couch and waited for the news. Images of the crashed helicopter came up, with the reporter's voice explaining what had happened. Then Meg's face was on the screen, along with the soundtrack of the few things she'd said. She'd expected that to be the end of it, but then the lights turned towards Colin as he stood among the trees by the river. Meg heard his sharp intake of breath.

'What? What are they *doing?*'

She had nothing to say to this and they watched in silence.

The reporter went on. 'We understand that Mr Peter Brown was first on the scene. The helicopter's engine was still running and the rotor blades were still turning. Despite the imminent threat of an explosion from leaking fuel, he broke a window to get in and turned off the engine. He probably saved the lives of the pilot and his passenger, but Mr Brown is a reluctant hero and chose not to talk to us about it.'

That was all that was said and then the report went back to the crash site and the people who'd gathered to watch, but Colin was looking very grim. 'That bastard agreed not to do this!'

Meg was surprised. Nothing he'd said had been used. 'Is there a problem? Your wife…?'

'No.'

'The police then?

'No, no.'

The report was continuing and some of the eyewitnesses were now on the screen. Meg turned it off. She waited for Colin to say something.

He spoke as if he was thinking it through. 'It's probably okay.' He continued as if reassuring himself. 'The camera was on me for less than a minute. It should be okay.'

'But is there some danger? Danger to you?'

'Possibly.'

It was clear to Meg that he wasn't going to explain any further. 'Well, I have little else to do these days. So if your life needs saving you can call on me.'

'I might just do that.'

It seemed as if he was trying to dismiss what had happened and whatever problem or trouble there was in it. He leaned a little closer and certain feelings began to stir in her.

Her voice was softer. 'Maybe we could have that kiss now at least.'

They were kissing on the couch and the kiss was lengthening when a key turned in the front-door lock.

It opened and Nick came in with his motorbike helmet under one arm and a small dog under the other. He looked at them in a way that was more cheerful than embarrassed.

'Er, sorry.'

Colin answered him. 'It's okay. I was about to leave.'

Meg didn't want him to leave, but she could hardly ask him to stay in the small flat now that Nick was there. 'I'll walk out with you.'

Once outside they could see the helicopter, on the level grass with a few lights focused on it, looking helpless and forlorn. Meg couldn't think of anything to say to Colin. Any possibilities between them seemed to have been thwarted by Nick's arrival. It was as if her life had just been put back into its proper context and they should probably say goodbye. She suspected that Colin was feeling the same.

She knew her voice sounded flat as she asked, 'Will I see you again?'

'It depends on which supermarket you go to.'

'Aldi.'

'I'm a Woolworths man.'

That sounded final but she couldn't let him leave without another try. 'Why didn't you want your face on the news?'

'Enough. I'll go now and I'll see you around. Maybe.'

She watched his dark figure as he walked up the unlit grassy slope towards his house. There was a streetlight in the turning circle so she could see him more clearly as he went over the crest of the hill and disappeared. He didn't look back.

She walked slowly back to her own flat where Nick seemed pleased with himself. 'I got a job today.'

'What is it?'

'Putting together scaffolding for a building company. It's only a week, but if they like me, they may keep me on.'

'What about the dog?'

'Can I leave her here? She's homeless.'

She considered this doubtfully. 'I'm not meant to have a dog here. Not without getting approval. It's in the by-laws.'

'You own the flat so they can't kick you out.'

'They could make it difficult for me, and I have to live here now. I don't want to be fighting with them.'

She looked at the little dog, who was a bitser of some sort with an untidy brown and white coat. She could certainly do with a bath and some grooming, but she also seemed like a dog with some style. Someone must have taken proper care of her once. She watched Meg with intelligent brown eyes. It was as if she knew somehow that this discussion was important to her.

'What's her name?' she asked.

'Bindi.'

'Bindi? Like the things that grow in the grass and hurt if you step on them?'

'Yeah, but it's also an Aboriginal name, a girl's name. My mate got a job overseas, and he was going to send her to the pound or even have her put down. So…'

She took a deep breath. 'Okay then. She can stay for now, but I can't promise anything.'

He looked at her fondly. 'I love you, you know, Mum.'

'I love you too.'

7

The whirring of a machine close by woke Meg early on the following morning. She was puzzled and even anxious for a moment until she realised that it was only Nick making himself a smoothie in the small kitchen. It was something that wouldn't have woken her when they were living in the house, but now she reacted to almost any sound. The events of the night before were coming back to her. She felt tired and off balance as she put on a shirt and jeans and went out to talk to him.

'You want a coffee?' he asked when she appeared in the doorway.

'Very much.'

'Sleep?'

'Not a lot.'

He made her coffee the way he knew she liked it – long black with a dash of milk – then made toast for them both.

'Have they said anything about your building on the news yet?' she asked him.

'What do you mean?'

'About you and others being evacuated because of cracks.'

He looked away. 'Maybe they haven't got a news crew to it yet.'

She considered this, then came to an uncomfortable conclusion. 'Did you make it up?'

He hesitated. 'Well, yeah. Because that guy was here. It would've sounded piss-weak to say I'd got kicked out.'

Her shoulders sagged. 'But you were kicked out? What happened?'

'The dog. They said I couldn't have her there.'

Meg knew it had to be more than that. 'What about the rent? I sent you the money. Did you pay it?' She understood that his silence meant he hadn't. 'You had a better use for it, did you?'

'Something like that.'

Meg decided not to push him any further. She was feeling strangely glad to see him. She took her coffee into the sitting room to watch the morning news and Nick followed. Soon the helicopter crash came up on the screen. The pilot was in intensive care but was in a stable condition. His nephew was expected to be released from hospital soon.

'Sounds like a lucky break for them,' Nick commented.

'What was lucky about it?'

'That you were around.'

'I guess so. Colin did the most.'

His face came up briefly on the screen once more and the reporter said again that he'd refused to be interviewed.

Nick was puzzled. 'Why not talk to them? What's his problem?'

'I don't know.'

'Makes him look kind of shady if you ask me.'

She couldn't argue with that. Colin's refusal to say anything was difficult to understand and might look in some way suspicious.

Nick looked around at her. 'What do you know about this guy? Colin is he? Tell me.'

She sighed. 'Well, he and I and your dad were at high school together. We were friends.'

'You mean he was your boyfriend? Before Dad?'

She nodded, aware that if she'd tried to disguise it, Nick would figure it out for himself. 'But then, when he turned twenty, he was called up for two years of national service in the army. He wasn't at university at the time or in a job that could have got him out of it. He had to go. The only other option was a military prison. He was in training first, then he did a year's service as a rifleman in Vietnam. And in that time…'

'Two years, you said?'

'Yes. Things changed.'

Nick looked at her curiously. 'You mean you swapped him for Dad?'

How simple that sounded, she thought, and how little it said about the pain she'd felt then and how it still lingered. The time she'd spent with Colin the night before proved that.

'Not straight away, no. Dad and I, we took part in some of the rallies together but…' It was getting too awkward to explain.

Nick considered what she'd said, then asked almost hopefully, 'This guy, he's not my real father, is he?'

She was amused by his question while still feeling the discomfort it caused her. 'No, he's not. All of this happened in the late sixties, long before you were born. Back then Dad and Colin were…best mates.'

'But you'd have married Colin if you could? Is that it?'

It was another hard question, especially coming from Leon's son.

'Well, things can always come unstuck but, yes, I think I probably would have. But if I'd married him back then, you'd never have been born.'

'A win-win for you.'

She laughed.

He looked at the time on the wall clock. 'I'd better go. I start work soon.' He stood up and the little dog looked up at him hopefully. 'Um, could you take Bindi for a walk? She needs to, you know…' He made a farting sound. 'Soon.'

'Okay. But, listen, I'd rather you weren't having to sleep on the couch.'

Nick considered this. 'Because I'll upset things with your new boyfriend? Old boyfriend, I mean.'

Meg sighed. 'Nothing will come of that.'

'If something changes, I can find another couch to sleep on. I've got a mate near here. He has three quarters of a shed out the back of his brother's place. I can stay with him for a few nights. Tell me when your boyfriend's coming over and I'll keep out of the way.'

'How do you have three quarters of a shed?'

He shrugged. 'Hard to explain.'

Meg was realising something. 'You quite like being homeless, don't you?'

'It's better than forking out huge wads of cash in rent to a slumlord with millions in the bank. Anyway, homeless people are more honest.'

It sounded true to her. 'And homeless dogs?'

'They're the most honest of all.' He headed for the door, then turned back. 'Living in these flats will be good for you, Mum.'

'Why?'

'Well, you spent much of your life trying to avoid people.'

'I did what?'

'I mean as a doctor. You can safely meet a few more of them now.'

This startled her, though she knew it was in some way true. 'Do these people include you?'

'Meaning did you avoid me? Yeah, I guess you did. It was because of your work though. Doctors have to keep at a distance, otherwise they'd never stop fixing people. There's not that many hours in a day.'

It was fair, she thought. 'Yeah, okay, that's been my life, but now it's different. I want my privacy, some quiet, and I think most people in these flats do too.'

He gave her a mischievous look. 'Things didn't seem so private when I walked in.'

She ignored this. 'Be careful on those big ladders.'

'I will be.'

The door shut behind him and after a pause she heard his motorbike start up. Would he ever be careful? She made herself another cup of coffee while Bindi remained alert near the door, her eyes following every movement in a way that told Meg she was hungry. There was no dog food in the cupboard, and Nick hadn't brought any with him. She could go to Aldi later, but in the meantime she had some chops in the fridge. She cut them up and the little dog gobbled them raw.

'Now you want a walk, do you?'

She wagged her tail enthusiastically. Meg clipped the leash to Bindi's collar and set off towards the river. There was a rising tide coming in from the sea. It made the river appear to be flowing inland.

'See this?' she murmured to Bindi. 'It's going the wrong way.'

Again she chose the path towards the golf club. There were a few players out already and she didn't want Bindi to get hit by a fast-moving golf ball. The path was still slippery in some places from the big storm, but she walked steadily along it in her rubber-soled shoes. The river was high and the smaller mangroves were submerged. Meg liked the mangroves and their strong earthy smell, and the way they grew with their roots exposed on the silt washed down the river. Above them the casuarinas on the bank were sighing in a light wind. She felt some easing of the dislocation and regret that she'd unleashed on herself by selling the house. She could walk down this path by the river whenever she wanted to and if she could keep Bindi, that would encourage her to do it.

The golf club café was open for breakfast, but Meg had drunk enough coffee for one morning, so she turned back along the path. She became aware of a young woman with a big dog coming up behind them. Bindi began barking and straining at the leash, seemingly intent on picking a fight with an opponent five times her size. Meg picked her up and held her while they went past and realised she was glad to be holding the little dog's small warm body. Yes, she should have a dog if she could, and Bindi would do better staying with her rather than couch surfing with her son.

Back at the head of the path, more work was going on around the helicopter. The rotor blades had been removed. People from the flats were watching, most dressed for work, and among them was a woman in her thirties in a tailored grey suit. Meg noticed the young mother she'd met the night before with her small son. He was clearly interested in Bindi.

She smiled at his mother. 'I'm Meg.'

The woman repeated it back to check that she'd got it right. 'Meg?'

'Yes. I was named after my grandmother. Her name was Margaret but she was always called Meg.'

'I'm Linh. I was named after my grandmother too. In Vietnamese it means spirit.'

'Ah. So does that mean you're not really here?'

Linh looked puzzled. 'What?' Then she realised what Meg had meant and laughed. 'I think so. I think I'm really here.' She looked at the little boy. 'And that's Teo.'

Meg felt she could safely let Bindi off the leash, and Teo began to play with her.

Linh looked at the people heading towards the station. 'I was the receptionist for a gym, the one above Woolworths, but I can't do it now. I don't have anyone to watch Teo.'

'Not your parents?'

'No. They weren't at all happy when he was born.'

A crane was hoisting the body of the helicopter onto a big truck. Several police on motorbikes were standing by to escort it. The woman in the grey suit came up to Meg. She was slim, with short and carefully-blonded hair, and her expression wasn't friendly.

'You're flat one, aren't you?' she asked.

Meg responded in kind. 'Yes. And you're flat who?'

'Four.'

'And I'm flat three,' Linh put in.

The woman seemed not to have heard her.

Meg was getting irritated. 'So we're all living quite close, aren't we. Don't we have names? Or are we just flat numbers?'

'My name's Suzanne.'

'And mine's Meg.'

Suzanne nodded to Linh but didn't say anything. Linh clearly resented this. 'And my name is Linh.'

Suzanne answered coolly. 'I know. Have you had any more trouble lately?'

'Not lately.'

'That's good to hear. Let's hope it stays that way.'

Neither of them explained to Meg what they were talking about, but she took it as a reference to Teo's dad.

Suzanne looked at Bindi, then at Meg. 'Is that your dog?'

'Well, no, not exactly. At the moment she's my son's dog, but I think she may be coming to live with me.'

'If she's his responsibility, I'd suggest you insist he takes her back. He should do it quickly, before she becomes attached to you.'

Meg shook her head. 'It's all right. If I do have her, I'll do it properly. I'll apply to the strata committee.'

'The committee alone can't approve it. The by-laws mean there has to be a vote of all the owners. I know some of them find dogs difficult and even intimidating.'

Meg was sick of this. 'Bindi's little. She might intimidate a cockroach but nothing bigger.'

'Well, we'll see. A recent application for a dog didn't pass so...'

Linh interrupted. 'But that was a big one. A Ridgeback or something.'

'A dog is a dog.'

Meg already disliked Suzanne. 'Well, that's a useful insight,' she remarked cheerfully.

Suzanne ignored this. 'There'll be a meeting of the strata committee within a few weeks. Put your application in writing and it'll go through the process. But don't count on a favourable response.'

She walked off as if the conversation was ended.

Meg spoke to her retreating back. 'I'm seventy-three, and if I want a companion animal, I don't see the problem.'

Linh was watching her little boy playing with Bindi. 'Neither do I.'

Suzanne turned back. 'You know the trouble with these small dogs? You go out for a while and the dog will bark and bark until you come back. Both the owners and the tenants get very sick of it.'

Meg had known this as a potential problem herself, but something else occurred to her. 'This place is full of cats. How did they get to live here?'

Suzanne shrugged. 'Cats are quiet.'

'Not in the middle of the night, they're not. Screeching and howling. Do you have one yourself?'

Linh jumped in. 'You do, don't you?'

Meg went on. 'And cats terrorise the small animals round here, don't they. Any bandicoots, baby possums or frogs.'

'I don't think we have any of those here.'

Meg raised her eyebrows. 'Don't we? Is it because they've all been tortured to death by the cats?'

Suzanne glared at her. 'I don't have time for this now. I have a ten o'clock meeting in the city.'

'You raised it, I didn't,' Meg pointed out.

Suzanne didn't answer and Meg watched her go, then turned to Linh. 'Is she always like that?'

'She's a lawyer.'

'Another one.' Meg was thinking of Jonathan. There were similarities.

Linh went on. 'She's on the strata committee of course. The men are all scared of her.'

Bindi turned away from Teo, braced herself and, with a look of concentration, shat on the grass.

Meg laughed. 'Just as well she didn't do that a minute ago.'

'Just as well.'

'And I forgot to bring a bag. This is my first walk with her.'

Linh found a plastic bag among her things and handed it to Meg, who scooped up the evidence. There were no bins around so she put the bag in her pocket, feeling its small warmth against her. Beyond them, the truck with the body of the helicopter was about to leave.

Linh watched it. 'I saw you get in to help those people when it was slipping down the bank. You were really brave. Will the hospital tell you if they're all right?'

'Probably not.'

They watched the big truck move out slowly. Meg put Bindi on the leash, said goodbye to Linh, then set off back towards her flat. As she went, she noticed Colin standing in the turning circle at the end of his street. He raised his hand to acknowledge her. Meg wondered if she should go up and speak to him, but would he stay long enough? She'd feel very awkward if she started to walk up there and he didn't wait. While she stood there undecided, he turned away, then went back over the crest of the hill and disappeared.

Once they reached the flats, Teo made it clear that he didn't want to be parted from Bindi. Meg invited them into her flat, made tea, then she and Linh sat on the balcony watching Teo with the little dog.

Linh returned to the subject of Susanne. 'Did you notice she made a point about me having trouble?'

Meg nodded. 'Teo's dad?'

'Yes. My parents had been keen for me to marry a Vietnamese man, but I didn't want to. There are too many... traditions.'

Meg knew about this. She'd seen patients with the problem of tight family control. 'Did your parents object to him? To Teo's dad?'

'Less than I thought they would. They even liked Adrian to start with. He paid attention to them and back then he had a trade. They didn't like him so much when I told them I was pregnant.'

'And then?'

Linh paused for a moment. This was hard to say. 'Ice. I mean ice the drug, crystal meth. It got to his brother first. This was after Teo was born. Then it got to Adrian.'

'Ah.'

'He started with a couple of pipes on weekends. It seemed all right at first…'

'But there's no safety catch with ice, is there? I've saw it in my practice. I'd have families I'd known for ten years with the kids doing well at school or wherever and then suddenly it was all gone.'

'It was like that with him. He was an electrician and he had a job when I met him, but when Teo was born things changed. Adrian decided to set up on his own. He said he wanted to do the best for his son and staying in the job he had wasn't enough. But then he had a lot of stress with the new business and what he had to do to keep afloat. He'd be up half the night with paperwork. He said the ice helped him concentrate and made it easier to get it all done.'

Meg sighed. 'I've heard that before.'

'He wasn't sleeping, then he had a meltdown here in the flats. That's what Suzanne meant. I think she called the police. He got four months in gaol, but now he's out again.'

'But not living with you?'

'I can't trust him. He'd take Teo if he could. Take him and disappear.'

'Have you got a Restraining Order?'

'Yes, but only for another few months. He can see Teo once a week, but another adult has to be there the whole time. I've got a friend who's helping me. She and Teo meet Adrian at the park and so far it's gone okay. He says he's off the ice but can I believe he'll stay clean? I don't know.'

Meg always found it hard to know how to respond. 'I really feel for you,' she began, 'but Teo has to be your first priority…'

Linh cut her off. 'I know, I know, and I probably shouldn't have told you all that. I'll take Teo home now.'

She got to her feet and grabbed the little boy's hand.

'Teo can come back and play with Bindi if I'm here,' Meg told her. 'And I'm usually here. I'm still settling in.'

Linh thanked her briskly, then took Teo back to her own flat down the corridor. It wasn't clear to Meg what she'd said to offend her, but maybe Linh had feared getting unwanted advice of the kind she'd hear from her parents. For the rest of the morning Meg attempted more unpacking. Nick had already filled most of the cupboards near the bathroom with his clothes and other stuff. She wondered if she should have said no to him moving in, but she knew in the end that she couldn't have done that. Jonathan could tell her all the bad stories he liked, but it made no difference. If Nick needed a place to stay, she'd always have room for him.

Later in the day she went for a walk with Bindi and thought again about Colin. Talking with him had brought back painful memories, including her guilt about what happened while he was in Vietnam, but there was something positive in it all too. She had rarely talked with Leon in the way she and Colin had done on the night at the golf club. It wasn't surprising, of course. Her life and Leon's had been focussed on practicalities – about the house, the garden, their work and so on. The things they enjoyed doing were often different but, as Meg saw it, they had always given each other space. She remembered how Leon's diagnosis had swept like a searchlight over their life together, illuminating all the things they'd been too busy and too practical to do. There was no way now to change any of that, but she did find herself wanting to see Colin again.

She remembered his street number, though she didn't want to turn up at his door, but the desire to see him persisted. She even shopped the next morning in Woolworth's in the hope she might run into him. But she didn't see him, and she couldn't hang around a supermarket all day. Next time she would shop at Aldi. She thought of writing a note to put in his letterbox, but that seemed desperate.

She was sitting on her couch and watching television in the early evening with Bindi beside her when there was a knock at the door.

She muted the television and called out. 'Who is it?'

'Colin.'

'You mean Peter Brown?'

'No, not tonight.'

She opened the door.

He came into the main room, then handed her a bottle of red wine in a paper bag. 'I was given this. I thought you might like it.'

She took it out of the bag, then noticed the label and reacted in some dismay. 'But that's Grange and it's worth…'

'Quite a lot, I know. I hope it's still good, not turned to vinegar. I've had it for years.'

'And no occasion to open it?'

'And I'm not likely to have one, so it's yours now.'

She didn't know what to say to this and settled for, 'Well, thank you.'

They looked at each other. There was a shelf on the wall where special items could be displayed. She put the bottle on it and indicated the armchair to him, though not the couch – that might remind them both too much of their interrupted kiss.

He didn't sit down. 'Is your son coming back tonight?'

'I don't know. He left this morning without telling me so I'd say there's a chance he might.'

'Then if I invited you back to my place, would you come? It's a nice evening and I'd walk you back later.'

She didn't hesitate. 'Yes. Okay. Yes.' But at the same time she wondered about his week-long absence and why, when she'd seen him, he'd turned away without speaking to her. She wondered too about the invitation to his house, but she didn't ask anything. 'I'll get a jacket.'

As she retrieved her jacket from her bedroom, she took a quick look at her hair, glanced at some perfume but rejected the thought. She picked up her keys and came back.

She pointed to the wine. 'Should I bring this?'

'Not unless you want to drink it all. Maybe keep it for an occasion.'

'This is an occasion. So, you really can't drink?'

'I have now and then over the years, one glass, even two, but I do better to leave it alone. As a doctor, you're not going to argue with me, are you?'

'Of course not.'

8

The streetlights were coming on as they walked together up the steep grassy slope, over the crest of the hill and down to his house. Meg looked at it with a feeling of unreality. It wasn't far from her old house or her present flat, but without the helicopter crash she might never have known Colin was living there. Would she have even recognised him if she'd passed him in the shopping street? Probably not. And he'd have let her walk by without speaking to her. His house was probably built at the time of the other workers' cottages. It had a wooden fence and a paved front yard with two big lemon trees that looked old and took up much of the space. The house itself was medium-sized, built of brick and had a corrugated-iron roof. Like other nearby houses, it had probably been built early in the last century but it wasn't rundown. The white paint on the windowsills was fresh and the house had clearly been looked after.

He opened the gate. 'The front garden was paved when I bought the place. At first I thought of digging up the pavement and planting more of a garden, but I didn't know what might be underneath – crushed stones, concrete and so on, maybe even asbestos – so I left it alone. It wasn't really worth the effort anyway. Most people with front gardens don't sit in them.'

'No, they don't.'

'But they're good for trees like these lemons. They were here when I bought it.'

The front door was at the far side of the house, allowing space for a narrow wooden veranda. As they went in, Meg noticed a heavy bolt and a second lock on the front door. Had they been left by a previous owner or had Colin installed them himself? If he had, she wondered why he needed them.

He showed her through the house. There were two bedrooms and a small study, a dining room with an oversized antique table and a living area with a comfortable-looking brown couch. There were pictures on the walls, most of them landscapes. She stopped to look at one in the living area that was of a twisted paperbark tree with distant purple and green hills. Meg thought she'd seen it somewhere before. Perhaps his parents had once owned it.

He took her through the kitchen, switching on the lights, and then out to the back veranda where there was a table and several chairs. The table was of dark wood, solid and well looked-after. The chairs were old too, and the seats were made of linen and looked as comfortable as armchairs. Towards the end of the long backyard, there was a big clump of tall trees. They looked to Meg as if they were at least a century old. Colin headed back to the kitchen and she followed.

'I've got some ordinary red,' he told her.

'Does it bother you if other people are drinking?'

'No, not at all.'

'Then, yes, I'd like some.'

He opened the wine, poured her a glass and got a soft drink for himself. 'It's warm enough to sit outside, I think.'

They went out to the back veranda again and sat in the semi-darkness looking out towards the trees. The tallest was an old white gum and there were more eucalypts, a spreading jacaranda and others she couldn't name.

She looked across the table at Colin. 'They're beautiful trees.'

'They're the main reason I bought this place.'

She was uncertain about the next thing she wanted to say but said it anyway. 'I thought you'd given up on me.'

He considered this. 'I wanted to, I really wanted to. Why revisit all that when it was so painful?'

'Yes. It was.'

'But the way we could talk that night by the river made a difference. You're also the only real connection I still have with…my past.'

'You didn't stay in contact with anyone else?'

'Not from school. Only some soldiers I knew from Vietnam, yes, but they kept on dying, mostly on purpose. A few got new lives and didn't want to be reminded of the war. I was close to my father… You'd remember him. But then he died too.'

He went on in a flat voice and Meg realised that the next thing was very difficult for him to say.

'You'd remember my younger brother too. He wasn't old enough to be called up, but he was killed the year after I left. An overtired truck driver veered off the edge on the Hume Highway and hit his motorbike. I couldn't even come home from the war for his funeral.'

Meg said nothing to this. 'I'm sorry for your loss' seemed to be the polite formula these days but he certainly wouldn't want to hear that.

He glanced at her, then continued. 'My world has grown smaller over the years. The closest person I have left is my daughter, and she has her own life.'

'The idea of Nick having his own life sounds pretty attractive.'

Colin laughed. 'Do you still have that dog?'

'Bindi. Yes, I do, though I may have a battle to keep her. There's a lawyer on my floor. She's got a cat herself, but she still seems determined to get rid of Bindi. She'll put pressure on the strata committee and also, I think, on the residents to vote Bindi out. I may have offended her, or else she doesn't want to set a precedent by approving a dog. Any dog. Whatever, she seems to have set herself up as my enemy. Mine and Bindi's.'

Colin was looking out over the backyard. 'I could have a dog here…'

'Yes, you could.'

'I'd like that, but I don't want to die and leave a dog. I don't know what would happen to him. Or her.'

Meg was startled. What was he saying? 'Do you have any reason to think you'll die soon?'

'Nothing physical.'

But she'd noticed his slight hesitation. 'Anything else?'

He paused. 'Not really, no. Other than being seventy-three. Like you. You can't conceal your age from me, my dear.'

She laughed. 'No, I can't.'

'Though you look younger. And of course the ideas about age have changed. Once you only made it to three score years and ten if you were lucky.'

'That's changed. But I guess I'd still…avoid a life lived out in a nursing home if I can. What about you?'

'Oh yes. I'd make other plans.'

She knew he meant suicide and she also knew there were worse ways to go. She looked out at the trees. A currawong in the tall white gum sent out a call that was repeated exactly by a bird some distance away.

Colin went on. 'I read a piece in *The Atlantic* a few years ago. The writer argued seventy-five was the right age for human beings to bring life to a gracious end.'

The idea startled her. 'Oh yes? That doesn't leave you or me much wriggle room.'

'He wasn't arguing for execution. It was simpler. He was saying that, after seventy-five, you shouldn't seek life-sustaining interventions such as pacemakers, defibrillators, by-pass surgery…'

The doctor in her was rebelling against this. 'What about cancer treatment? Antibiotics?'

'As I remember it, they were included.'

'And what if you and I are still wantonly alive at the end of another two years?'

He laughed. 'I like "wantonly alive". And, yes, I'd like to think that we'll be wantonly alive at the end of two years, but you never know.'

The way he'd said it left Meg wondering if there was something about the state of his health that he wasn't saying, but the evening had been peaceful so far and she felt she shouldn't pursue it. Instead she asked him to tell her about his daughter.

He seemed relieved by the change of subject. 'She's nineteen, and she and her mother both live in the mountains, though separately now. She shares with friends.'

'What does she look like?'

'Well, more like me than like her mother. Lucy's fair and blue-eyed, but Beth has my dark hair and eyes. She's a thinker and can upset people by speaking her version of the truth, though she never intends harm. Good people understand that.'

'So she takes after you, does she?'

'Good people like her more than they like me. And now she seems to be making a life for herself in the mountains. I've mostly stayed, when I could, around the Inner West.'

'We didn't ever move away from it either.'

'You and Leon?'

Meg nodded. She was thinking that maybe she shouldn't have mentioned Leon. She turned to look at Colin's face to see if it had bothered him. His expression seemed calm in the muted light.

'I saw him again,' he said. 'Soon after I got back. I suppose he told you about that, did he?'

She was surprised. 'What? No.'

'We met in the Cross and went to the Bourbon and Beefsteak Bar for a drink. He wanted to tell me he was sorry about what happened with you while I was gone. He said he'd keep right out of the way if I asked him to.'

Meg absorbed this and the fact that two men were planning her life for her back then without her knowing.

She felt strangely resentful. 'You didn't toss a coin for me, did you?'

'Not quite.'

'Pissing contest?'

'Not that either.'

There was still an edge to her voice. 'So what did you say?'

'I didn't say anything. I stood up and punched him hard in the jaw. I would have landed it better, but I had to lean across the table. His chair went over or I would've done it again. A couple of Yanks grabbed me but I got free and punched them too. As far as I was concerned, any Americans deserved it after the war. Then the cops came… Didn't Leon tell you all this?'

'No, he didn't. He was in the emergency department one night but he said it was just a bar brawl. He didn't tell me it was you. Did the cops charge you?'

'They were going to because I'd started it, but then Leon said he didn't want to press charges. The two Yanks weren't going to bother. But I decided Sydney wasn't a safe place for me. The winters were too cold in my snore-and-vomit boarding houses. So I headed up north.'

Meg took this in. 'What did you do there?'

'This and that. I couldn't stick to anything for long. I guess I was like Nick.'

'I think there's a difference.'

'Maybe, maybe not. His generation's got it hard, though in a different way from us.'

Meg knew she should probably leave the subject of Leon alone, but there was something she needed to say. 'Leon felt guilty about it too, you know. Like I did. You'd gone to Vietnam and he hadn't just because his birthday wasn't pulled out of the barrel. That, along with the war itself, was very cruel and arbitrary and so we went to the protest marches.'

'And that was exciting, was it? You felt like you were really achieving something. You'd go out and have a drink afterwards and feel a real rush. And later in the night you'd end up in bed together, or I suppose, knowing Leon, in his dad's Ford Falcon?'

It hurt, but what he'd said was accurate enough. 'That's it, more or less. And then we'd both feel bad about you, and we wouldn't see each other for a while.'

'At least not until the next protest march… And the next fuck?'

She looked down.

'Did either of you ever get arrested?'

'I did once. So did Leon. We were in the middle of the city, in Martin Place. The arrest seemed quite ordinary and not particularly frightening at first, but then I was put on my own in a holding cell and left to wait. The time seemed to go on and on with no indication of if or when I might get out of there. That scared me the most.'

'I'm sure it did.'

'Leon was in a holding cell with other guys further down the corridor. They talked and laughed together so he didn't mind it at all. Then we both had to go to court, but all we were charged with in the end was obstructing access to the men's toilet in Martin Place. It was the only thing we'd done that was illegal. We hadn't even realised we were doing it.'

Colin laughed. 'We didn't get to hear much about the protests, you know. The officers protected us from news in general.'

'I suppose they would.'

'But we did hear that people were booing and spitting on returning soldiers when they got home and had to march through the city streets.'

Meg was quite shocked. 'Really? I don't think so.'

'No, it wasn't true. We were later told that people came out of the shops and offices to celebrate, and there was ticker tape as well. But even so, most of us agreed that we were somehow to blame. That all we'd been through, the pain, the constant fear, the loss of friends, didn't count.'

'That wasn't true either.'

'No, I don't think it was, but it's how we thought about it. Not many of us marched on Anzac Day. Even among other soldiers from the two world wars we felt unworthy and unwelcome. It was as if we'd been killing people for no reason, not defending our homeland in the way they had.'

'Did you ever march on Anzac Day?'

'Not for the first ten years or so. And after that I had another reason not to.'

Neither of them said anything. Meg could hear the last calls from the birds as they settled down for the night.

'It's getting late,' she said. 'I should go home, I think.'

'I won't ask you to stay. But we could have coffee or go out to dinner, like I was wooing you. If that appeals to you of course.'

'Are you? Wooing me, I mean?'

'I don't know yet. And I think it's best I don't know. For your sake too.'

She stood up ready to go. 'It was good to see your place. I like it, and especially the trees front and back.'

He stood too and looked at her. There was a new gentleness in his voice. 'I'll walk you home.'

The evening had remained clear and cool, and a light wind carried the salty smell of the river towards them as they walked together over the crest of the hill and down the steep slope on the other side. Lights were on in the flats and each one of them looked small and separate.

'So your son's living with you again, is he?' Colin asked.

'For the time being, yes, he is.'

'And that's how it will be from now on, will it? You gave up a bigger place you could both comfortably share for a smaller one that you can't?'

She reacted angrily. 'Yes, I did...' But then she decided there was no point – he was right anyway. So she said, 'But I'm not minding it much now.'

He seemed surprised. 'Aren't you?'

'Nick and I fit together quite well. He comes and goes and he's got some work. He's in construction. And everyone else, my friends, the ones I want to see anyway, have moved out of the city. We email each other about keeping in touch but we don't really.'

'Tell me more about Nick.'

'Well…' She didn't find this easy. 'I was forty-three when he was born. Before that there'd been a late miscarriage, a girl.'

He nodded and she knew he was hearing the pain in her voice. It never went away entirely.

She went on. 'I'd wanted another child if I could manage it. Leon seemed to agree, though he left the decision to me. I tried things, including fertility prescriptions, but no other pregnancy followed. Then, when we were both in our early forties, I was unexpectedly pregnant with Nick. I've loved him all his young life, and I love him now but…' She didn't go on.

Colin picked up on it. 'Do you want to explain the "but"?'

She answered reluctantly. 'My idea of what a life should be and his are…different. He's good at lots of things and yet he couldn't settle on anything. He set up two of his own businesses but they didn't work out, mostly for reasons that weren't his fault. He can't seem to stick at any job.'

Colin nodded. 'And he's probably smarter than the people above him in the jobs he's tried. I was like that too.'

'Were you?'

'Yeah, I got jobs easily, but then I'd start to think the bosses and supervisors were doing things the wrong way. I'd see them screwing over people who didn't deserve it. But instead of trying to deal with them, and given that they'd always win, I'd quit. Often just before I got fired. My life has worked out anyway, sort of. His might.'

'I hope so.'

When they reached her door, Colin only touched her shoulder and then walked off.

9

Meg let herself into her flat and straightaway noticed the smell of cigarette smoke and something else she couldn't identify. Nick wasn't there, and in any case he didn't smoke, so she thought maybe it was from another flat. Then she noticed that the Grange that Colin had given her wasn't on the shelf. She heard a key turn in the lock and waited with growing suspicion. Nick came in and Bindi danced happily around him.

He noticed his mother's dark expression. 'At least someone's pleased to see me.'

'Where is it?' she demanded.

'Ah, well…'

'Where is it?'

He gave up. 'I sold it.'

It made no sense to her. 'I don't believe you. It was only given to me a few hours ago. Did you drink it?'

'No, of course not. I saw it here and I knew you wouldn't drink it on your own. I knew you'd let it sit there till it turned to vinegar…'

'It was given to me!'

'Yes, and I mean to split the profits.'

'But…'

'I got a buyer straight away. He's been and gone.'

That was the cigarette smoke. 'What would you have done if I'd come back while he was here?'

'Introduced you, I guess. His name's Bunt. I don't know his other name. Don't you want to know how much I got for it?'

Wearily she asked, 'How much?'

'Fourteen hundred. Where did you get it from anyway? I presume you didn't shoplift it from a bottle shop.'

'Colin gave it to me.'

'Oh. Okay. Him. I thought he'd done a runner.'

'I didn't tell you that.'

'You didn't have to.'

Meg sat down heavily on the couch and Bindi leapt up to sit beside her. She didn't know how to handle this. She'd let him share the flat – she had almost welcomed him – and this was the result.

'I looked up the year of this one,' Nick was saying. 'Grange 2010. It's listed at $2,999.99.'

'Is it really?'

'Yeah, one cent short of three thousand. How could you drink it once you knew that?'

Meg didn't attempt an answer. As well as the cigarette smoke, she identified the other smell as a sickly-sweet aftershave. It was like fruit salad left too long in a bowl. It didn't seem likely to her that someone known as Bunt would wear this kind of aftershave, but apparently he did. She opened all the windows, although it was getting cold outside.

Nick watched her. 'You're really angry with me, aren't you.'

'Are you surprised?'

She was remembering the opioids he'd sold out of her medical bag. It seemed that nothing had changed.

'I'm sorry.'

'No, you're not. Cancel the sale.'

'I can't. You don't cancel a sale with someone like Bunt.'

'So it's like it was with my medical bag? Once the stuff's gone, you can't get it back?'

The answer to this was obvious. Instead he asked, 'Do you mind if I put some toast on?'

Meg didn't object so he went into the kitchen and she followed. There was something she'd never raised before with him. 'Nick, tell me this. Clearly and truthfully.'

He was putting bread in the toaster. 'What?'

'Are you on ice? You know, methamphetamine?'

He wheeled around to look at her directly. 'No, Mum.'

'Then why did they kick you out of the flat? It can't only be because of Bindi and the rent being a few weeks overdue.'

He stood by the bench and concentrated on buttering his toast. 'It was about the payments on the motorbike. I couldn't handle the rent as well.'

Once more her shoulders sagged. The wretched motorbike.

He went on. 'But my mate, the one with the shed, is moving to Queensland soon. He thinks his brother might let me take it over.'

'I thought it was only three quarters of a shed?'

'Maybe four fifths.'

Meg felt exhausted. Too many plans, too many uncertainties. The toast was buttered and Nick reached for the single avocado in the fruit bowl on the table.

This was too much. 'Leave that fucking avocado alone!'

He backed off, then came over and put his arms uncertainly around her. 'Oh, Mum.'

He seemed to be half-expecting her to push him away, but she let him hold her while telling herself that at least it wasn't ice. But at the same time she felt a new kind of despair. Colin was right that she and Nick were in a place too small for them both. And what would she tell him about the Grange? That she'd drunk it on her own?

She and Leon had allowed small evasions to creep in between them – not lies exactly but evasions. She didn't want that to happen with Colin. She'd talked to him honestly so far. If anything were to happen between them in the longer term, she wanted to maintain that level of honesty. She could buy another bottle from the same year and put it on the shelf, but it would be an evasion, and an expensive one, though she could demand some of the cost of it from Nick. She was too tired to sort it out so she left him spreading crunchy peanut butter on his toast and went early to bed.

The matter of the wine was uncomfortable, but in the end Nick was her son. Colin was a former lover, with the complexity of their whole adult lives behind them both. But she still remembered how hard it had been all those years ago when she'd seen him off on the troop ship.

She remembered the uneven boards of the pier under her feet, the smell of the sea, the cries of the gulls and all the sad farewells going on around them. She remembered how afraid for him she'd been and how deep her sense of loss was once he was gone. All the same, it would be hard to reconstruct anything with him now and she risked him ending it at any time. But if he did, she would still have Nick, and also little Bindi who was helping her new place to feel like something of a home.

She remembered Jonathan's advice about selling the house and dislodging Nick. It hadn't worked out too well for her yet, although it had meant she was close by when the helicopter crashed and she had, for better or worse, met Colin again. Better or worse, which was it?

Next day it kept troubling her until she'd almost decided to replace the wine before Colin came back, but then he was unexpectedly at the door. As before, it was early evening and he didn't call her in advance. She let him in uneasily, noticing that he'd had his hair cut and was wearing what looked like a new blue jumper. They remained standing and, as she'd feared, his eyes when straight to the shelf where the wine had been.

He looked pleased, assuming that she'd been drinking it herself. 'Did you like it?'

She thought for a moment of telling him she'd put it away in a cupboard for a special occasion – he wouldn't go and check – but again she felt they'd begun with a level of honesty and it was important that she keep it up.

She answered in a flat, neutral tone. 'I didn't get a chance to like it. Nick sold it.'

He looked at her with a puzzled frown. 'What? Really?'

'Yes. I'm sorry. He did it in the time I was up at your place.'

She felt her face flushing hot. Already she was regretting not having replaced it when she could.

But Colin smiled, then laughed. 'If he sold it that fast, the man's a genius!'

'It doesn't…?'

'Worry me? No, it was probably the best thing to do with it. It was presented to me when I retired. Someone who didn't know much about me thought it was a good idea. It's better that it's out of the house.' He could see Meg looked unconvinced. 'Truly, don't worry about it. I'll think of a better present for you sometime. I came to ask if you'd like to go out for dinner.'

'When?'

'Now. That's unless you have no other plans.'

She found Colin's relaxed familiarity both welcome and unsettling. It took her a moment before she answered. 'No other plans.'

10

Passing headlights reflected off the front window as Meg slid into a seat in a Chinese restaurant. It was large, carpeted and quiet so Colin wouldn't have trouble hearing. A waiter came and took their order. Meg looked around, reminded of several times when she'd been there before and had noticed a tall man who sat reading by one of the windows. His face was always turned away and even when he was leaving and walking to the counter to pay, he hadn't looked towards her. Could it have been Colin?

She waited until the meal arrived and they ate more or less in silence, then she began hesitantly. 'Part of the problem, for me at least, was that you were gone so suddenly. We had no chance to talk or make plans.'

He shrugged. 'Because they scooped us up and sent us south to that dreaded place, Kapooka.'

She knew it was difficult for him, but she persisted. 'And it was ghastly?'

'Of course.'

'Can you tell me?'

'Do I need to?'

'It's part of my history too.'

He seemed reluctant still, but he answered. 'Well…the first five or six weeks were sheer hell. From the dark early morning, they pushed us very hard all day. A lot of it was just brutal and illogical. Like we'd have to go with packs and all our stuff through a deep, freezing creek when there was a bridge close by.'

'Why would they do that?'

He shook his head. 'I dunno. Some idea of shared hardship uniting us against the enemy. We had to understand fast that the only way to survive was for us to stick together. And in the end we more or less got it. We were even friendly with some of the NCOs by the time we were shipped out.'

'But you had leave before you went. You didn't try to see me then.'

'Yeah. I had a few days, but I was afraid if I saw you I might decide to go AWOL. That would've meant years on the run, maybe for us both. I couldn't have done that to you.'

He looked at her to confirm this and she nodded. No, she wouldn't have.

'Or else it was a couple of years in gaol. We don't have a Canadian border to slip across like the Americans did.'

'But after your two years were up and you came back…'

'And realised…?'

She shook her head quickly. 'Let's not talk about that. I just want to know what you did.'

'First I went back to Sydney Uni, though I kept well clear of you…'

She cut in. 'I wasn't even seeing Leon then. We didn't link up again until after I'd graduated and done my intern years.'

'I know.'

'But you could have talked to me.'

'It was too hard to be near you and Leon. And too hard after Vietnam. It was so quiet and safe back here, like nothing had changed. But I had.'

'That's a depressing picture.' And wrong in its way, she thought, but she understood why he had seen it that way. 'And of course the protests were still going on.'

'Oh yes, they were. I was going into a lecture and someone stuffed a flier into my hand about the next protest. That was the day I gave up and walked away for good.'

'And went north?'

'Yeah, and I did this and that. It wasn't till I was well into my thirties that I came back to the Inner West. I took a job with a company that made parts for choppers, small aircraft and boats too. It was boring, but I didn't have to think much, and I liked the people. Some of the older ones had been in the Japanese war, and a couple of them had been in Vietnam. We didn't talk about it. But it was easier because everyone understood. It was stable enough for me to ask Lucy to marry me, and later on Beth was born. That was the big thing. That baby girl made my grip on life much stronger.'

'Grip?'

He nodded. 'It's been tenuous since I got back, as it was for others too. I've told you that. But Beth made it worth it, when she was little at least.'

'But not now?'

'Time will tell.' Colin was looking out through the window at the cars passing along the dark street. He turned back and went on as if with some effort. 'Lucy and I… Well, it was a bit shaky from the start. Then things happened. We often had to move house.'

'And your name…changed.'

'Yeah, but I was already Peter with her.'

Meg took a deep breath. 'Are you going to tell me why?'

'Maybe another time.'

'Or maybe not' was what she heard in his voice. Of course things had happened in the past fifty years that they'd each want to keep to themselves. Things about Leon and herself, yes, and presumably things to do with Colin or Peter and his wife.

They sorted out the bill and got an Uber back to Meg's flat.

Colin kissed her at the door. 'Is he inside?'

'I don't know. He uses my hidden keys to get in, then puts them back.'

He frowned. 'Meaning you keep them on the top of the door?'

'No, it's more sophisticated than that.'

He looked down at her. 'Well, if you and I ever get some time alone…'

'Time alone?' she asked.

'Time alone.'

She felt old sensations begin to move within her. He kissed her again lightly and walked away.

Meg felt that something was at last becoming both steadier and clearer with Colin, and she slept better that night. In the morning there was a knock at the door and Meg opened it, hoping it might be him. It was Linh, who asked hesitantly if Meg could possibly take Teo to meet his father at the park. The friend who usually took him had called in sick with COVID.

Linh looked pale and anxious. 'I can't go myself. I'm not supposed to because of the court order, and I can't deal with Adrian anyway. But if no-one turns up, he'll report that I broke the agreement, and he'll take me to court again. You don't have to do anything, just make sure he doesn't take Teo.'

'When is he supposed to be there?'

'In half an hour.'

'Okay, I can do it.'

Linh's face brightened with relief. 'I'll get him ready.'

As Meg prepared to leave, she began to think about what could go wrong. If the Iceman, as Nick had begun to call him, tried to steal Teo away, she wouldn't have the strength to stop him. Calling the police would take too long. Even shouting and making a fuss wouldn't work. There would only be babies and grandmas this time of day.

Then she saw Leon's hammer on the kitchen bench, where she'd left it after putting up a few pictures. She picked it up and felt again how heavy it was. A solid workman's tool. Her handbag was also on the bench and she slipped the hammer into it. Having done it, she felt rather silly. It was too much. She took the hammer out, feeling the weight of it in her hand. It might not help the situation, but what else could she do if she had to? She put the hammer back in her bag.

Adrian was already waiting by the swings when she arrived with Teo. He seemed unconcerned when she told him that she was filling in for Linh's friend, but Meg knew from experience that, if he was still on ice, the situation could change at any time. All the same, she wanted to believe that after everything this rather nice man had gone through, he had learnt something and might take up his life again, either with or without Linh and Teo. Nearly half an hour went by without trouble, but then Adrian stood up.

'There's a service station just down the road. I'm going to take Teo there to buy him an ice cream.' He looked at his son. 'What do you think, buddy?'

Teo looked hopeful, but Meg was alarmed. 'Linh said you're not supposed to leave the park.'

'It's barely a hundred metres away.'

She reached instinctively into her bag and felt the smooth timber surface of the hammer. 'I think we should stay here.'

He put his hands up as if trying to calm her. 'Okay, okay. No need to reach for your phone.'

She quickly withdrew her hand from the bag.

11

The rain started and seemed like it would never stop. Colin came to see Meg several times, usually in the afternoons, and they'd walk back to his house together. They'd sit on the back veranda looking out at the trees, sometimes not speaking for a while. It signalled a change from the past weeks when so much had been said. She was there with him one evening when she thought of the afternoon of her nineteenth birthday.

They'd met together in the same small upstairs room at the People's Palace, to which they'd gone whenever they could afford it. She remembered it clearly because it was the day the condom broke. They had both stared in dismay at the pieces of it, then Meg had gone down the corridor to the women's bathroom, knowing that it might already be too late. It was a time when abortions were still illegal. Would she have wanted one anyway? No, she wouldn't have. But they were both nineteen. It would be very hard to finish her medical degree and internship with a baby. Neither of them had the money to pay rent, but it would not be at all comfortable to live with either of their parents.

Two weeks passed and Meg thought about little else. Then one morning it became clear she wasn't pregnant. She was deeply relieved but also a little sad, like she had been robbed of an alternative future that she had let herself imagine.

Night was falling on the veranda. She looked at Colin. 'Do you remember the day the condom broke?'

'What?... Yes, I do.'

'If I'd been pregnant...?'

He didn't hesitate. 'We'd have got married.'

'Yes, we'd have had to back then. And there's something else as well. It would have saved you from Vietnam, wouldn't it?'

He reflected on this for a moment. 'Yes, it would have.'

'Could we have managed? I couldn't have continued studying medicine.'

He was emphatic. 'No. I'd have got a job, any sort of job. I wouldn't have let you drop out of uni.'

She knew it was true. Whatever happened, he would have stuck by her. She said, 'And then your number was picked out of the barrel...'

'But, I'd have been a married man with a child on the way. They wouldn't have taken me.'

'Maybe we should've got married quickly when they first announced the Birthday Ballot, then tried to get pregnant.'

'Maybe we should have. But I think we still believed in luck back then.'

It was all too hard to think about. The different choices they could have made back then. The different lives they might have lived.

Her thoughts turned again to that day at the People's Palace. 'When did you buy that condom? Do you remember?'

He considered the question. 'When I was about fourteen, I think. Or maybe fifteen.'

She laughed. 'You were hopeful then?'

'Yes, I was.'

'And it stayed in your pocket all that time? No wonder it broke.'

There was a pause, then he held out his hand to her. 'Maybe we can just lie down together…?'

'Sounds like a good idea to me.'

'I can check if I've still got one of those old condoms.'

She laughed and shook her head.

They walked through the dark house to his bedroom and Colin turned on the lamp by his bed. It was an unusually warm evening. The window was open and the white linen curtains moved gently. They took off all their clothes in silence and lay down on the bed – a very comfortable one, she noted. She was self-conscious about how much older she was now, and she noticed the scars and ridges on his chest.

She ran her fingers along his scars. 'They look bad.'

'I was helicoptered out and they worked fast.'

'They must have. They're long scars. You could have…' She stopped.

'But I didn't.'

They stayed holding hands and then he began to move very slowly and somehow it all worked. And she remembered again more clearly how things had been between them all those years ago. Not much seemed to have changed.

They lay together afterwards and she felt the wind cool on her naked body.

They stayed quiet for a while and then he asked, 'Would you like to stay the night?'

She hesitated. She was beginning to feel she'd rather like to go home and have time to pull back and think about what had just happened.

He seemed to sense it. 'It's okay if you want to go.'

'Well, Bindi was on her own when I left, though she was fed and had her litterbox. Nick may be back by now. I don't know. But whatever, you don't need to walk me home.'

'Okay. I think I might sleep now.'

'You still have trouble sleeping?'

'Oh yes, I do. But it's not only the dreams. They trained us to wake at every sound.'

'I'm sure some of it still feels like yesterday.'

'Maybe the day before yesterday.'

She let herself out of the house and set off to walk the short distance over the hill and down to her flat. The streetlights were on above her and she could smell the mown grass on the golf course and hear the night birds calling from the river.

Back in the flat, Nick looked at her expression and smiled to himself, but didn't comment. And so it began and went on. She and Colin would eat together either at his place or hers, or else go out to a local restaurant, usually Chinese or Vietnamese, and then either go to bed together or not. There seemed an easy consensus about it between them. They each needed some days to pass before they attempted making love again. Their bodies were ageing but that didn't seem to matter much. They were with each other and both seventy-three and they probably had some time ahead of them.

At home one morning Meg was unpacking another box when she came across the same article in *The Atlantic*. It was the one that argued against taking action to extend one's life past seventy-five. The writer's name was Ezekiel J. Emanuel and she wondered if it was a pseudonym to avoid angry protests from readers who wanted to live longer. She looked him up on her laptop and saw that it was indeed his name and that, like her, he was a doctor. She checked his age and saw he had quite a few more years of life ahead of him than she did. She gave up on the boxes and decided to take Bindi for a walk. The small dog seemed to her to be something of a mind reader. Meg only had to think of the word 'walk' and Bindi would be at the door ready to leave.

She thought more about the article as they headed down towards the river. Dr Emanuel had mentioned 'outliers' to whom his theory didn't apply. She hoped, as she assumed most people probably did, that she and Colin would both prove to be outliers. Her life seemed suddenly more solid and purposeful now. Was she in love again? Whatever the truth of it, and however it turned out, he had made a difference already.

Over dinner that night at the same Chinese restaurant, Colin asked her, 'Are you still sorry you sold the house and bought the flat?'

She considered this. 'Only in the sense that I'm in a smaller space, and it's a bit overpopulated by Nick and Bindi being there as well, but I'm finding I don't mind much now.'

'Well, if it's a problem, you can always move in with me, if only for a break.'

She looked at him, startled. 'Do you mean that?'

'Yes, why not? The place is big enough. You can have your own room, and a study if you want one.' He went on, leaning back in his chair. It was as if he was changing the subject quickly so she didn't have to answer yet. 'But there's one thing I haven't told you. In 1998, I went back to Vietnam. Only to the north, the south was too…familiar. I wanted to see who we'd been fighting and why. Quite a few soldiers did that.'

'How did you find it?' She was feeling both stirred and a little unnerved by his casual invitation to move in with him. She'd made so many changes in these past weeks that she didn't feel ready to make another, even if she wanted to.

'The Americans had bombed it all into the ground,' he told her, 'but it still looked old and like nothing much had happened. Hanoi was a busy French city with lakes surrounded by trees that looked like they'd been there forever. The buildings were narrow and French, with stairs that led up to apartments and little balconies.'

'Was it how you'd thought it would be?'

'No. The whole place was much bigger than I'd expected. All these people getting on with their lives despite the hell that had rained down on them.'

'Did you only go to Hanoi?'

'I went by overnight train to the Chinese border. Up there the hill tribes still farmed the old terraces. Some of them were living a day's walk to the nearest road. I liked those people and I stayed with them for a bit. It suited me to be away. Despite everything, it's still wild and beautiful. I could take you there sometime, that's if you'd like to go.'

Another invitation. Meg found she couldn't answer it yet. 'Did it feel like you were among…' She hesitated.

'What, among the enemy? Not really. My tour guide was from the military police, but otherwise no. I was glad to see, at least where I was, that the ordinary life of the people still went on.'

The streetlights were on as Meg and Colin finished the meal and set out to walk back to his house. The air was growing colder and they walked quickly and without saying much. Meg was still adjusting to the two invitations she'd got in the last half hour. She was pleased that he'd made the offers, but also uncertain. Was she quite ready for all this?

They reached Colin's front gate, and Meg, who was closest to the letterbox, noticed that someone had stuck a wedge of shiny paper into it while they were away. It appeared to be a screenshot of Colin standing beside the river. A message was written across the paper in thick black letters – *Nothing has changed. I know where you are, Peter Brown.* She reached out for it, intending to pass it to Colin.

He grabbed it first and shoved it in his pocket. 'It's just junk mail.'

She was puzzled. 'Are you sure? It's got your other name on it.'

He didn't answer. He was staring at a man sitting on a motorbike at an intersection further down the hill, his face hidden by a crash helmet. It was at a point where another street intersected with Colin's and continued on towards Meg's own flat. Colin still stared at the man. It was as if he was preparing himself for danger, and he looked to Meg like the soldier he had once been. The man revved the motorbike loudly a few times, then rode off.

Colin glanced round at her. 'Come inside.'

He opened the front door for them both, and she followed him as he went through to the kitchen and took a bottle of whisky from a cupboard. He poured some for himself and indicated the bottle to her. She shook her head.

She couldn't help asking the obvious question. 'Sorry, I know it's none of my business but should you be doing that?'

He put the bottle away. 'I won't keep doing it, if that's what you mean.'

He drank the whisky in silence, staring out a window that overlooked the backyard.

Even if he wanted her to, she felt she couldn't ignore what had just happened. 'Who was that on the motorbike?'

'I've never met him. Don't even know his first name.'

'And yet he was watching you.'

He turned back to her. 'I can't do this tonight. I mean, I can't talk to you about it. Sorry, but I think you should go home.'

'Do you expect him to come back?'

He shrugged. 'You shouldn't be here if he does.'

'Okay then.'

She went towards the front door, picking up her handbag from the chair near it. She'd left it on her way in.

He followed her. 'And it's better if I don't walk you home.'

'Why? Because he might see me with you?'

'Yes.'

'It's all right. It's hardly any distance. I'll be fine.'

But she was hurt and, although she knew she probably shouldn't be, she was offended too. Colin might make love to her, and even suggest that she move in with him, but he couldn't tell her about the meaning of the screenshot in the letterbox or the handwritten line. Did he realise she'd read that line before he grabbed it away? She went in silence out the front door, down the steps and out to the street.

She looked around and called back. 'He's gone.'

Colin was standing in the open doorway.

'Well…goodnight then.'

He didn't answer. She went on past the big lemon trees. They seemed to smell stronger in the dark. She reached the gate and wanted to look back, maybe wave goodbye to him, but she didn't. It was all too strange. Earlier that evening he'd asked her if she might want to come and live with him. It was clear that wasn't going to happen now, but he wouldn't tell her why. It only took her five or so minutes to walk home, and when she unlocked the door she found Nick lying on the couch and watching TV with a sleepy Bindi beside him.

He was surprised to see her. 'I thought you'd be out somewhere with your boyfriend.'

'No, and maybe not anymore.'

'What happened?'

Meg wasn't sure that she should tell Nick, but she felt she needed to talk to someone, anyone, about what had just happened.

He switched off the TV. 'Something wrong?'

'Yes, something's wrong.' She hesitated again, then sat down in the armchair, took a deep breath and explained, 'We'd been out for dinner. When we came back, I noticed something in the letterbox. Colin said it was junk mail but it wasn't. On the night of the helicopter crash, a television crew had started to film him as the hero, which in fact he was. He told them to stop and said they couldn't use anything he'd said. But they had a close-up shot of him standing among the trees by the water. They used that.'

'Did he get anything in writing from them?' Nick asked.

'What the hell would it matter now?'

He nodded sagely, clearly thinking that Colin should have had the sense to get a written contract. Meg wondered if she should stop there but, against her better judgement, she told Nick about the message that she'd read – *Nothing has changed. I know where you are, Peter Brown.*

Nick absorbed it. 'That's a threat.'

'And then I saw a guy sitting on a motorbike watching us from the intersection. You know where I mean?'

'Below Colin's place, yeah.'

'The man had his helmet on so I couldn't see his face. He stayed there watching and then he rode off.'

'What sort of motorbike was it?'

'What?'

'Was it a Yamaha like mine? Or a Harley Davidson or a Triumph or a Suzuki…?'

'I have no idea. Why does it matter?'

'The engines all sound different.'

'Well, I don't know about that. All I know is that Colin suddenly changed. He made me go home.'

'So what's he not telling you? I mean, could he have been in gaol? Maybe he was part of a bank robbery and cheated the other guys? They saw his face on TV and found out where he lives.'

Meg shook her head. 'None of that sounds right to me.'

'But it's how long? Fifty or more years since you last saw him? He could've done anything in that time.'

Meg thought about it. Logically Nick could be right, but it seemed to her that it went deeper than being chased by ordinary criminals over an ordinary crime.

'You need to ask him, Mum. Make him tell you.'

'I need to wait a bit, I think.'

He shrugged. 'Up to you. You're an adult, aren't you?'

'There's some evidence for that.'

'It's called life.'

She groaned inwardly. Did she need her stay-at-home son to explain life to her?

12

Almost a week had passed since Colin had hurried Meg out of his house without telling her the reason. She could have phoned him, but what happened that night was so strange, and so absolute in its way, that she thought she should leave the next move to him.

She was out with Bindi for her morning walk. There was a kind of buzzing in the air as if bees and other insects were welcoming the sunlight and the warmth of spring after the long rainy winter. She reached the intersection where she'd seen the man on the motorbike. She hesitated, then decided to walk up the hill to Colin's house. From the footpath, it seemed closed up and silent, but she had a feeling that he was inside. She went through the gate, between the lemon trees and up the steps to the front door. She knocked and waited, then saw a shadow move behind the spyhole.

She called out, 'It's only me.'

He opened the door. 'Okay, come in. Hello, Bindi.'

He seemed very tired and there was laundry piled on the couch.

'Can I take Bindi out the back?' she asked.

He led the way through to the veranda with the tall and watchful trees beyond.

'Tea? Coffee?' he asked.

'If you want some.'

'I'll make coffee.'

She sat in one of the deep chairs and waited, and he brought out the coffee.

'Colin…?'

'I know, I know. Like many things, it goes back to Vietnam. I was in a platoon where our own lieutenant had been injured and was recovering at the base. He was replaced by a sergeant who was Australian but had spent time with the Americans. He'd adopted the American view that you just kill anyone you suspected of being Vietcong, as many as you could. The idiot seemed to think that if you wipe out enough innocent people, the soldiers will stop fighting. We knew it doesn't work like that. But, at least for a while, he was our commanding officer.' He drank some of his coffee.

Meg waited in silence.

He continued. 'We kind of managed him for a bit, calmed him down when he was going off his head. But then we got a tip-off about the people in a village on one of the mountain slopes. They were supposed to be storing weapons for the VC, a lot of weapons. These tip-offs were often bullshit. Sometimes they were just local vengeance, maybe for an unpaid debt or some other feud. But the sergeant said we had to go up there.'

Colin paused again, drank more coffee, then went on. 'It was a steep climb and the ground was boggy. There were no tyre tracks or other signs of the heavy vehicles you'd need to get serious weapons up there. The houses in the village were all made of bamboo with nothing you could lock up. But the sergeant was determined to interrogate the villagers. All the younger men were away working, so he picked on an old man holding a baby. He demanded to be shown where the guns were or else he said he'd burn the village. It turned out that he'd brought a little jerry can of kerosene, and he shoved it in the man's face. The old man didn't understand and kept backing away. Then he turned and ran, still holding the baby.'

Colin was speaking calmly, like he'd said it before, but Meg could see tears pooling in his eyes.

'The sergeant ran after him, yelling at him to stop or he'd fire. The old man didn't stop and the sergeant shot him in the back.'

Tears were now running down Colin's cheeks, but he continued. 'The old man was so skinny that the bullet passed right through him and killed the baby too. He kept firing pistol rounds into the air and telling us to round up all the village people. The fucking idiot was making all this noise and standing out in the open, no cover at all. He kept waving his jerry can around. Then there was incoming fire from the ridge above us, and more from the nearby jungle. The VC must have heard the shots and come to have a look at what was happening. The rest of us found a bit of cover beside the path so we could return fire. But the sergeant took a bullet in the chest and fell down next to his jerry can.'

Colin stopped as if it was too hard to go on.

'He died?' Meg prompted.

'Yeah, though not straight away.'

'But why's the motorbike man angry with you. He was out in the open, and they were shooting at you?'

'It turned out the bullet was from an Australian rifle. It didn't really mean much. Our guns were better. The VC stole them from any of our men who'd been killed, and we always carried lots of ammo.'

'So anyone could have shot him?'

'Yeah. But then there were…differing accounts.'

Something in the way he'd said this puzzled her. 'But why you? No-one else?'

'I was a few yards ahead of the rest.'

'But you didn't…?'

He took in a sharp breath. 'No, I didn't. And I was one of the men who carried him back to base. He was alive and seemed all right. But then he wasn't.'

'Others could have fired the shot though, couldn't they?'

He nodded. 'We all hated the stuff he did, especially the nashos. We were different from the regulars. They'd chosen the army and we hadn't.'

'But what's this got to do with the man on the motorbike?'

'He's the sergeant's son.'

There was a pause. 'But why…?'

'There were three men in the platoon, regular soldiers. They told our commanding officers that they saw me turn my barrel towards him after we all hit the ground. It led to a military hearing. There was contradictory evidence and there were no findings. But the son's been stalking me for years.'

'But the inquiry said you were innocent?'

'It didn't really. It was left open because of the lack of evidence. And he was quite young when his father died. Maybe only nine or ten. He didn't start coming after me until he was older. I changed my name and moved. He found me and I changed it again. This last time he hadn't found me for a while.'

'But the news crew did.'

He nodded. 'I'd begun to think it was too dark for me to be recognised. And my face was only on the screen for half a minute.'

'But it was enough.'

'And the timing. To get close to you again, close enough to suggest you move in here and then…'

'But why would he do anything to me? I wasn't in Vietnam.'

'You matter to me.'

Meg looked out at the trees. Two magpies in the white gums were calling to each other as if in conversation.

She turned back to Colin. 'But you didn't kill him?'

It seemed to take too long for him to reply.

'No, I didn't.'

She looked at him, thinking that if he was going to lie about anything, he would lie about this. And maybe he had good reason to. But he held her eyes calmly and she saw in him the man she'd been beginning to love again.

'Can't the police do anything?'

'Not until he does something worse. Like he murders me or he attempts to. Something on that scale.'

'But they could arrest him for stalking, couldn't they? Couldn't you take out a Restraining Order?'

'As you probably saw in your practice, Restraining Orders don't work with anyone who doesn't care. If I did bring in the cops, he might persuade them to get the inquiry into his father's death reopened. There's no time limit, not on murder. I don't want that.'

'Then can't you confront him and convince him you didn't do it? Have a lawyer with you or something?'

'I don't know his first name or where he lives. His father's surname was Williams. After Smith and Jones, it's the third most common surname in the country. Google will tell you that we have a hundred and five thousand of them. How would I track down the son with nothing more than his surname?... More coffee?'

'Yes, I think it's justified.'

He went into the kitchen and, after a pause, brought back more. They sat drinking it in silence.

Colin spoke quietly. 'This is my problem, Meg, not yours. Maybe I should've told you all this before I became…entangled with you again. At least given you proper warning.'

'Should you?'

'But nothing had happened since I moved here six years ago. I'd begun to think it was over. I didn't know those TV arseholes would rat on me.'

'I want to be entangled with you. I don't really see why this should keep me away.'

'But listen…'

She cut him off. 'No, you listen. The risk doesn't seem all that great to me. Is this man really going to pour kerosene on us while we're asleep? Burn down the house with us in it?'

He looked amused. 'I hadn't thought of that, but it's not a bad idea.'

She gave him a quick smile. 'But does he have kids? A family? Would he want to spend the rest of his life in gaol? He wanted to scare you again, yes, and he did that, but so far I don't see any more to it.'

'Remember I'm not dealing with logic here.'

'No?'

'And it's why I don't have a dog.'

'Meaning he could…?' She looked at Bindi, sniffing at the base of a tree. 'But what about getting a big dog? One that'd bark at night if he came near you?'

'A big dog can be poisoned. I don't even have a budgie.'

She laughed. 'Okay, then Bindi stays at my place. It's still a little crowded with her and Nick so I'd like to be able to come here. I'm an adult, as Nick says. It's up to me, isn't it?'

'If you were here at night, I'd be awake all the time listening for motorbike engines.'

'My place is possible too.'

'I'd rather get to know your son a little better first.'

That was fair enough, she thought. And like Leon, Nick had a way of asking direct questions. He might not be too tactful with Colin.

There was one more thing for her to say. 'I think you should install a security system at least. You know, with cameras, motion sensors and so on. You've got those extra locks on the front door but they're not really enough.'

'Ah well…'

She interrupted. 'I can help with this, you know.'

'What do you mean?'

'Help pay for it.'

'No, I can do it. And since you insist on forcing your way in here, then I certainly will.'

She laughed. 'Yes, I'm forcing my way in. My decision, okay?'

They sat together for a while and talked about other things. It seemed to Meg that they were both trying to return to some sense of normality, but she also knew that, with an unknown and vengeful man who was coming after Colin, it wouldn't be easy.

13

Meg didn't see Colin over the next few days while he arranged the cameras and other protections. It didn't trouble her. It seemed that, having revealed the threat to her, he was taking it more seriously himself. Then he came to see her, unexpectedly as usual, one mid-afternoon. In his jeans and a dark grey shirt, he seemed tall and fit and formidable even at seventy-three. He sat as usual in the armchair while Meg took the couch, which, she noticed, already had a few muddy stains on it. He told her that the cameras and motion sensors were now in place.

'So do you feel safe?' she asked.

'I'll get used to it.'

'Maybe safe enough to have me there at night?'

He hesitated. 'I guess so.'

'You don't sound convinced.'

'I'm not. One thing I do know about this guy is that he was, or maybe still is, in the SAS.'

'Special Air Service?'

'They know what they're doing.'

'But how do you know he used to be with them?'

'He effectively said it in one of his messages. He wanted me to know that he had the training to follow me wherever I went and take me out without a gun. Unlike me.'

'Why unlike you?'

'A gun was the way I was supposed to have killed his dad.'

She took this in. 'That's pretty scary. Do you...'

'Have a gun?'

'But do you have one? Licensed or unlicensed, I don't care.'

He gave her a sideways grin. 'You should care, but no, I don't have one.'

Meg wasn't sure how she felt about his answer. If the man on the motorbike was truly intent on killing Colin, then what? She'd rather he had a gun.

She asked a different question. 'Do you know how old this man is?'

'If he was, say, nine or ten when his dad died – and I don't know for sure – then he'd be in his early sixties now.'

'Old enough to get over it?'

'Maybe.'

'But he still rides a motorbike?'

'Yes, a Triumph. It's been the same one all along. He always revs it loudly to make sure I've heard him. He knows I'll recognise the sound.'

'Nick tells me that each make of motorbike has a different one.'

'They do.' He looked at her. 'Have you talked to him about me?'

'Back on that first night when you made me leave, yes, I did. I felt shocked at what had happened, and he could tell that. He knows me well.'

Colin considered this. 'So Nick is in the loop now.'

'I haven't told him much and he hasn't asked questions. As far as Nick's concerned, I make my own choices. So does he. He's not judgemental and he wouldn't object to anything that's happened with you so far.'

'But if I got his mother killed he might?'

She laughed. 'Yes, he might take a dim view of that. Listen, he could be back soon unless I text him to stay away.'

'Ah, so you have a kind of alarm system of your own set up too.'

'I do, so could we go for a walk? Change our location?'

'Where to?'

'Along the river?'

'Sure.'

Something occurred to Meg as they walked together out of the flats. 'At least we know that with all the new alarms and cameras, this man can't get into your place unseen while you're away.'

'True.'

But she could hear uncertainty in his voice that told her that he wasn't wholly convinced. They walked on towards the river and, in a silent consensus, took the path to the golf club. Puddles and muddy patches had been left on the path by rain the night before and a few trickling streams crossed it. Once again Colin put his hand lightly on Meg's arm. The day was mild and sunny and the river was flowing towards the sea as the tide went out. The water was brown, but where the sun caught the tiny waves stirred up by the light wind, it glittered silver. As they walked, Meg was still trying to think through what he'd told her.

'If this man is in his early sixties, he's probably not still in the SAS, is he?' she asked. 'That's if he ever was.'

'No, probably not.'

'But there should be records, shouldn't there?'

Colin shrugged. 'Does the army reveal the names and addresses of SAS soldiers to anyone? I doubt it.'

Meg was still thinking about it. 'We can assume the man had a tough time as a kid because he lost his father, but there was probably more in his childhood too that makes him keep tracking and threatening you. Maybe his dad treated him badly. Perhaps very badly. His mother might well have left. He could have been raised by grandparents or even in foster care. All these things count.'

He looked at her sideways. 'So you're taking it upon yourself to unpick it all, are you?'

She recognised the resentment in his tone and felt embarrassed. 'I'm sorry. I mean that. I've spent a lot of time asking about people's lives and trying to solve their problems, so it's something of a habit. Are you telling me to keep out of yours?'

'Out of my life? No, not necessarily. It's actually good to be able to talk about it. It was always possible that he'd find Peter Brown sooner or later.'

'Was it? You could at least have moved interstate.'

'I could, but I needed some kind of continuity, I suppose, and so I wanted to be back here in the Inner West. I thought he'd still be hard put to find me here. I also didn't want to be too far from Beth.'

'I don't think those news people understood what they were doing. The helicopter crash was a big story late in the day. They didn't use anything you said.'

'They still had my face and name on the screen.' His tone changed. 'But it's done. We are where we are, as they say. And it's good that I've got the security stuff, even though I'm not sure it would stop him.'

'But still worth doing?'

'I might even get some sleep.'

Her next question was important to her. 'So you're not moving on? Not getting a new name just yet?'

'Not today.'

There was something about him that seemed to her deeply resigned, even defeated. It made her ask, 'But I've got the story straight, have I?'

'How do you mean?'

'There was an inquiry. If you weren't exonerated, at least you weren't charged. But he still believes you're guilty.'

'Yeah. All of that.'

'But if you didn't fire the shot, do you know who did?'

'All of us hated what the sergeant had done, and he was about to start a fire. He didn't give a shit about shooting the baby and the old man.'

'And it can't have been a bullet from the Vietcong?'

'Yes, it could have been. They'd clearly been watching for long enough to take up positions on two sides. The whole encounter only lasted seven or eight minutes and then they disappeared. Can we…?'

'Stop talking about it? Yes, of course.'

There was almost no wind in the trees by the river and the fish weren't jumping. Some tiny birds flicked over the surface of the water.

'Do you know if Captain Cook came up this river?' she asked him. 'I know he sent a naval longboat up here. I don't know if he came himself.'

'He might have. He was a nosy fellow. He might have wanted to see what this river was like.'

Meg looked again at the brown water flowing steadily past and thought of the pelican who often sat under the road bridge on the opposite side. She thought of him as 'he' because he seemed old and wise and had claimed the rock platform as his own. The shadow of it in the daytime and the streetlights at night would probably help him to catch passing fish.

'Have you seen the pelican that often sits here?' she asked.

'Yes. I know him well.'

'And do you know the Aboriginal name for the river, Goolay'yari, means pelican?'

'Of course I do. It's always been a pelican river. I live here, remember?'

She accepted the slight reproach. 'So he'd be descended from the pelicans who were already here when Cook arrived.'

'Yes, he would.'

It occurred to her that Colin was himself like the pelican – self-contained and watchful. But, unlike the pelicans, he had an underlying well of anger.

She thought of one more thing she needed to ask him. 'Where do you keep your car?'

'I've got a mate who owns a repair garage. It stays with him and he locks it up at night. But other than that, there's not much more I can do. I need to wait until Mister Williams or whoever he is breaks the surface, and then do whatever has to be done.'

'But then you can deal with him, can't you?'

'You mean stop him from killing me?' His voice was weary. It was as if he was ending the conversation. 'I'll give it a go.'

He left her at the bottom of the hill and set off for his house while Meg walked back to her flat. Colin's new protections might make a difference, she thought, but she knew from her own experience that someone determined enough could probably still get to him. Her GP surgery had been broken into several times by people who were never caught, despite cameras and alarms. She wished she could do something more, but without the man's first name and with a common surname, he'd be difficult to track down. Maybe too difficult.

Next morning she decided to try to ignore her continuing unease and take some time for herself. She booked a haircut, walked to the shops and stayed for lunch. Her phone had gone flat and she couldn't find the charger so she left it behind.

14

Meg returned to the flats after her morning out, but then noticed that her car wasn't in its usual parking space. Her first thought was that Nick had taken it. She checked her hiding place. Her spare house key was there but the key to her car was gone. She assumed Nick had taken it and it annoyed her. It seemed that he'd could always find something to do that would get to her. But the handwritten note propped against her fruit bowl proved that it wasn't Nick. It was Colin.

The note he'd left read – *Emergency in the mountains. Beth in hospital. My car's locked up at my mate's garage but he's away. I couldn't find one to rent today. I tried to ask you but your phone wasn't answering. I'll call as soon as I can.*

Meg retrieved her charger from under a pile of Nick's clothes and plugged it in. While her phone recharged, she moved restlessly about the flat, always staying near enough to it to answer a call. She could phone him, but he'd said it was an emergency and she didn't want to intrude on that. It was mid-afternoon before he called.

He was trying to talk against many background voices. 'Beth's been in a car accident…'

'Oh no!'

'But they're telling me she'll be all right. They should even be able to release her soon. But it was a very near-run thing.' The background voices interrupted him. 'I can't talk properly here. I'm at the hospital and there's too much noise. I'll call back when I can find a quieter place. It might take a little while.'

It took an hour and a half. During this time Meg mostly walked around carrying her phone, followed by Bindi, who seemed to know something was wrong.

The phone rang. It was Colin.

He said, 'Beth was delivering flowers to someone in Wolgan Valley. It's on a narrow winding mountain road. Someone on a motorbike forced her off the road close to the escarpment. She managed to steer into a small tree, which stopped the car. The rider on the motorbike went straight on.'

'After the accident?'

'Yes.'

They were both silent, and then she asked, 'The police were called, I take it?'

'They've seen her in the hospital. They wanted to know if she could identify the make and colour of the motorbike. They showed her a series of photos, but Beth said she was trying to avoid hitting the rider and she wasn't really looking at the bike itself. The police asked if the rider could've been a woman but she didn't think so. It seemed to her that it was a man. Quite tall.'

There was a pause, then Meg asked, 'Do you think it was him?'

'I don't know.' Colin sounded wrung out, exhausted. 'He's only just found out my current name so it's a long stretch to think he'd straightaway go after Beth.'

'Why?'

'She's got a different surname from me. And since Lucy knew Peter Brown was a cover, she used her own name for herself and for Beth. It made sense. But if he did have her name and where to find her, yes, he'd come after my daughter.'

Meg felt the shock. 'Does Lucy know about this?'

'Yes, and she's all fired up about it being my fault. She won't leave Beth's hospital room, and it's awkward for the two of us being there together. I'll come back soon. You'll need your car anyway.'

'No, I won't. I hardly use it.'

'I think I should come back. The tension with Lucy's not good for Beth. I'll be able to see her when she gets out of hospital. She may stay with Lucy for a little while, she says, but then she'll go back to the share house. It's nearer to the university.'

'Are you worried about that?'

'Not really. If it's him, he's probably done what he set out to do. Not to kill Beth, but to give me a big scare.'

'I guess so…' Meg wasn't entirely convinced.

'And if it's not him but some idiot riding too fast round a bend, then there's nothing much we can do except wait and see if the cops pick him up.'

'Did you tell them what we know?'

'I told them that a man named Williams rides a motorbike and has a grudge against me going back to

Vietnam, but I had no proof it was him. They wrote it down, but I didn't get the feeling they'd do much about it. How can they really?'

'I think we need to find out who he is and maybe get a lawyer in on it.'

'So I do what? Get a private investigator to try to find him? That's possible... Look, I'll be back tomorrow morning. We can talk about it then.'

Meg didn't hear from Colin in the morning but she assumed he couldn't use his phone while driving. It was hard to concentrate on anything else so she went out to sit on the balcony to wait with her phone in her pocket and Bindi on her lap. By midday she still hadn't heard from him. She'd begun to have a bad feeling, so she wasn't much surprised when her phone rang and it was a police officer, a woman.

She gave Meg her name, Detective Saunders. 'We need you to come down to the station.'

Fear engulfed her. 'Is it something to do with my son?'

'No, it's not.'

She breathed again. 'Can you tell me what it's about then?'

'We'd rather talk to you in person.'

'I don't have my car at the moment. I'll have to get an Uber.'

'We'll wait.'

~

The detective was older than Meg had expected, with tightly drawn-back hair. A young male constable was with her and was preparing to record the interview.

'Am I suspected of something?' Meg asked.

'No, not you. But we do need to record a statement.'

'A statement of what? Why do you need to record me?'

'You told me on the phone that you didn't have your car at present. We need to know if it was stolen or if you gave permission to someone else to drive it?'

A cold feeling was coming over Meg. 'Why?'

'Stolen or taken with your permission? Which one?'

She took a deep breath. 'It was taken by a friend of mine. I wasn't there at the time but he left a note. It was a family emergency.'

'So you didn't know beforehand that he was taking it?'

Meg felt increasingly uneasy. Where was this heading? 'Not at the time, no.'

'So in legal terms, what would you say? Either that it was stolen or it was borrowed with your permission?'

She already knew she should probably say it was stolen, but she couldn't do it. 'I'd have let him take it so, yes, you can say it was taken with my permission. He was going to a hospital in Katoomba to see his daughter who'd been in an accident. When we spoke later on the phone, I told him that I didn't mind him having the car.'

'So you're confirming you gave permission for him to use it?'

Meg nodded.

'I need you to say it for the record.'

'Yes, I did.'

'Then I have to tell you that Mr Brown was in a multiple-car accident early this morning on the western freeway. An accident that, so far at least, it appears that he caused.'

Meg found it hard to breathe. 'Is he all right?'

'Yes, he is. Minor injuries. Same with the drivers in the other cars. But you're saying he's known to you and he was driving the car with your permission?'

Why did she have to keep repeating it? 'Yes. But I've got insurance, both third-party and for the car itself.'

'I'm afraid he was intoxicated.'

'Oh.' Meg looked down at the bare table. 'But he never drinks.'

Saunders went on in her clipped manner delivering the bad news. 'He was drinking the night before, it seems. Apparently he set off from Katoomba at about five-thirty this morning. He may not have realised he was over the limit. He also admits he was driving tired, without sleep. You can argue it with your insurance company, but I think they'll be reluctant to pay up.'

Meg breathed deeply. 'How many cars were involved?'

'Three as well as yours.'

'Has he been charged?'

'With drink driving, yes, but he'll be released now we've spoken to you and established that the car wasn't stolen.'

Meg could hear a certain sympathy in the detective's tone. The young officer clicked off the recording machine in silence, then got up and left. Detective Saunders remained at the table sorting through a few papers but said nothing more. Meg waited for a few minutes, then gave up and walked out too.

She came out into the cool fresh air. Light rain was falling and she didn't have an umbrella. She didn't know much about Colin's financial situation, but he didn't give the impression that he lacked money. It didn't trouble her too much either way. She had money left over from the sale of the house, though it was meant for her to live on into the extended old age that Ezekiel J. Emanuel disapproved of. At least the accident didn't sound too bad. Everyone was alive and not much hurt. Repairing cars might be costly but repairing people was harder.

It occurred to her that Colin could have his phone on again, but she had no idea about how it would all play out between them. She decided to text him – *I've talked to the police. They'll let you go soon.* She wondered if she should add 'Love, Meg' or an X for a kiss, but she decided to send the text as it was.

The thing that troubled her most in all this was the alcohol. Colin would have been deeply shaken by his daughter's near-fatal accident, and most of all by the question of who or what had caused it. But was the drinking only a brief relapse or was it likely to continue? He'd spoken of himself and Meg as being 'tangled up' again. It was accurate and she'd welcomed it, but had she been wrong? How far could she trust him if he was drinking again? She might get a clearer sense of it when they saw each other, but for the moment the accident made her question her feelings for him. Everything seemed suddenly to be on hold.

His answer to her text came in – *Thank you for not dumping me in prison for car theft. Will catch the next train back. We can talk then. In the meantime you need to know that I will pay for all of this, and that I'm sorry, truly sorry.*

She got an Uber back to the flat with an older driver who seemed to sense that she'd lately had some bad news. He spoke to her in a kindly way and told her a few stories about other passengers he'd driven. It helped, but as she unlocked the door to her flat, she felt most of all that she needed a drink. She recognised the irony in this. Beth had been run off the road close to the escarpment. Was it any wonder that Colin had felt he needed a drink, then another one, then a few more after that?

Bindi welcomed her, jumping around happily. Meg picked her up and hugged her, glad she was there. Then she poured herself a strong brandy and mineral water and sat on the couch with her arm around Bindi to wait. She had another brandy and wanted a third, but she'd need to talk to Colin soon and she shouldn't do it too much affected by alcohol herself. She watched the news channel where the same stories came round each half hour, but she didn't know what else to do. She knew the train would take a while, then he might go home, have a shower and put on fresh clothes before he came to talk to her. Would he have a drink before he did? He might.

Much was uncertain, but she knew that one part if it wasn't. If the motorbike man, Williams, had caused Beth's accident, then he had to be found, confronted and dealt with. It had to happen fast.

15

It was almost two in the afternoon when Colin finally knocked on Meg's door. He looked to her as if he'd come directly from the train. That was something, she thought. He came in, and she indicated that he should sit in the armchair again while she took the couch.

'Are you all right?' she asked.

He laughed. 'Well, no, not really.'

'So talk to me. Did you get hurt?'

He spoke calmly, like a soldier dealing with an incident. 'I got a little banged up. Mostly bruises. A few cuts. Minor stuff.'

'Ambulances were called?'

'Yes, but no-one needed them, and the drivers in the other cars were good about it all.'

'That's lucky.'

'Yeah. Three guys on their way to work. There were a few minor injuries, which was why the cops were called. Whiplash might still turn up too.'

She knew about whiplash. It often emerged in the days after an accident and was difficult to treat.

'How's Beth?' she asked.

'She was improving when I left. I could see it'd only increase the tension for her if I stayed.'

It didn't feel to Meg like a time for tact. 'So you went out and got drunk?'

'Yes, I did.'

'Very drunk?'

'Moderately, I'd say. I was still very shaken by what had nearly happened to Beth. And I kept turning the same question over and over. Could it have been him?'

'Could it?'

'I don't know. Neither do the police. But yesterday afternoon I drove to the place where she'd gone off the road. She was driving the flower-shop car. You remember? Her part-time job?'

'Yes.'

'The car was still there. Close to the edge of the escarpment and up against a small tree. A sapling really. It looked like it could still give way and the car could go over. But at least there weren't any houses below, only forest.'

Meg shuddered. 'Scary.'

'A tow truck arrived. A guy on his own. He backed up, hitched the car to a chain, then he pulled it back onto the road. He did it as if this kind of thing happened all the time.'

'Maybe it does.'

'Maybe. Then he nodded to me in a friendly way and drove off. I went back to the hospital until it got too uncomfortable with Lucy. Then I had to leave. I'd had no sleep since the accident. I thought I should book in somewhere before I drove back. I saw a pub that let out rooms and thought that would do. And it would have, but…the bar was still open.'

'Ah, I see.'

He went on defensively. 'My daughter had nearly died. My heart was still racing. I thought I could handle one drink, but then…'

'A second and a third?'

He nodded. 'I just couldn't calm down after what had happened.'

'I know that well enough.'

'I tried to sleep, but I kept waking up. About five in the morning, I got up and made myself a couple of instant coffees. I thought I was okay to drive. I wanted to get the car back to you. And I wanted to see you as well.' He paused. 'It didn't occur to me that I might still be over the limit.'

'The coffees were part of that, were they?'

He nodded. 'I'd say so. And I wasn't much over.'

'But it was enough.'

'I have to appear in court in a couple of months.'

'You'll plead guilty?'

'What else? I *am* guilty… Can we go and get something to eat?'

They made it to the Chinese restaurant just before it closed for the afternoon. They were let in by a woman in charge, and then took seats by a window as usual. Meg felt glad they had the restaurant to themselves.

Colin looked across at her. 'You're taking the drinking as a sign of things to come, are you?'

She answered honestly. 'I'd thought about it.'

'But seeing me now, how does that make you feel?'

She looked at him steadily. 'I don't think I can give you an answer yet, but I also feel it's the kind of thing that could've happened to any of us. It's why the police do breath tests in the early morning. To catch people on their way to work after a big night out.'

'So you've seen it before? As a doctor?'

'I had a patient who did it. I went to court on his behalf, but they still took his licence. Driving was essential for his work and he lost his job. He was in his fifties and he couldn't get another one.'

The woman came to take their order and left.

Meg and Colin looked at each other. The hardest questions seemed to have been raised already and partly answered.

Colin moved on to more practical matters. 'Well, at least I'm not working and I don't have to drive. You can have my car for the time being. As long as it's tucked away under your building, there's little risk of Williams seeing it there.'

'I don't really need it. I still have Leon's car parked in the street. I start it up now and then to preserve the battery.'

'You don't drive it?'

'I have only once. There was too much of him still in it for me then.'

Colin seemed to understand this. 'I'll get your own car fixed up with the rest. There'll be some panel beating, but I was well within the speed limit.'

This too was a relief to her. If he'd been speeding while tired and over the limit, it all could have been much worse.

'And you said Beth doesn't remember anything much about the motorbike or the rider?'

Colin shook his head. 'It was dusk, her last delivery and she only remembers a flash of red and silver. She knew she was close to the escarpment so she was concentrating on how to stop the car. A rock, a tree, a solid bush. Anything.'

'And she found something.'

'And saved her own life. I'm really proud of her.'

'You should be.'

'But she was dazed, possibly concussed. She said the small tree was creaking and bending, threatening to break. She managed to fall out onto the ground with her phone, then tried to call the police. The call wouldn't go through, and she found a stick and walked slowly uphill to a point she could call from, scared all the time she'd collapse on the road.'

'She's a brave girl.' Something else occurred to Meg. 'I know it'll sound like an odd question, but did she say what the flowers were? The ones she was delivering?'

'It's an odd question but, yes, she did. A dozen long-stemmed red roses.'

'For someone's special celebration then.'

'Since they didn't make it, she asked me to ring the shop and get more sent over.'

'I think I'd like your daughter.'

'I think you would too.' He said nothing for a moment. 'What now?'

'You should go home and get some sleep. You've got the cameras to protect you.'

He hesitated as if not sure he should ask this yet. 'Will you come with me?'

She knew she needed to back off and have time to think about it all. 'Not this time.'

He paused and looked at her. 'I'm thinking of selling the house.'

'Where would you…go?'

'I might buy a flat like you did. Something in one of these big anonymous blocks around here. Somewhere I could disappear.'

'So not far away?' She could hear the relief in her own voice and assumed that he could too.

He smiled at her. 'No. As long as you're still speaking to me.'

'You'd change your name again, would you?'

'Not hard to do. And I don't need to go far from here. It's only a matter of covering my tracks. I'll change my bank details and so on, but it can be done.'

Meg liked his house and would be sorry to see it go. 'I suppose so.'

'And I don't get much mail other than the threatening sort these days. I'll go home and sleep if I can, but could we meet again sometime this evening? Perhaps at the golf club? There's more to say.'

'What more?' What else could he need to talk about so soon? It was already the middle of the afternoon.

Colin shook his head. 'Not now. I need to get some sleep first. But could we meet for a drink, a lemon squash, at the golf club this evening?'

She agreed to this. The waiter brought their food and they ate their very late lunch in silence. What Colin meant by 'more to say' hung in the air. It made her impatient and uneasy, but she felt she shouldn't press him anymore this soon after the accident.

He went home to sleep and she walked back to her flat. Nick wasn't there – he had more work with the scaffolding people. She went out and sat on the balcony with Bindi beside her.

~

As the sun began to set, Meg walked alone down the path beside the river, heading for the golf club. The path was slippery again because of showers during the day and she missed Colin's arm supporting her. It took her a while, but she got there and saw him at a table in a quiet corner.

He stood up as she came over. 'Would you like a drink?'

She hesitated. 'No, not yet.'

'So we do this cold turkey, do we?'

His tone was stiff and she could tell he really wanted a drink but was holding out because of her. She didn't answer. They both sat down but neither said anything. The silence extended and she wondered if he wanted her to ask questions. She decided not to. He had something to tell her and there was nothing else to talk about until he did. He glanced around as if to make sure he couldn't be heard, then spoke softly.

'I did kill him. I mean, I did shoot him.'

Meg nodded but said nothing. She'd tried not to guess what it was he was going to tell her, but once he had, it felt like something she had known all along.

Colin went on, speaking rapidly. 'At least I think I did. The sergeant was out in the open and screaming at us to move forward and return fire. But it was all so confusing. Some of the shots were coming from the jungle and others from the ridge. He risked getting us all killed. I think I raised my rifle towards him by a few degrees. The regular army guys say I did, though I don't think any of them could really know. But I believe I did it, although I'm not entirely sure.'

Meg's voice was very flat. 'So you lied to me.'

'Yes. I agonised over it. I knew it'd come down to a yes or no answer, but more than anything I didn't want to burden you with knowing.'

'Did…' Her voice cracked and she had to clear her throat. 'Did you think I'd dob you in?'

'It wasn't about that, but I did…fear telling you. There are certain things you can't unknow about someone.'

She nodded. That was true. She was feeling a new and painful sense of dread through her whole body.

Colin went on. 'All the rest of it was true. The sergeant was brutal. He couldn't see anyone on the other side as a real person. Not even the old man and the baby or the other people in the village. It was like he was in a shooting gallery.'

'Why are you telling me this now?'

'Because Beth's accident has changed things. It's no longer in the past. It's very much in the present and decisions need to be made. They should be based on the truth of it.'

She considered this. 'Would you ever have told me otherwise?'

Again, he leaned his elbows on the table and dropped his face into his hands. 'I don't know.'

Meg nodded and looked away, thinking it through. She saw Suzanne arriving in the bar with three other women.

Colin had more to say. 'Do you know what fragging means?'

It took her a few moments to think of it. 'Isn't it the deliberate killing of one of your own officers?'

He nodded. 'There were two hundred and twenty known cases with the Americans, and probably more that were never revealed. The term came from fragmentation grenades, which were seen as the easiest way to do it.'

'And you did,' she said quietly.

He went on. 'We'd been ambushed and everyone was firing, firing almost at random. Though I hated this man, I hadn't thought of doing it before but…' He paused.

'But?'

'I think I raised my rifle slightly and turned it towards the left. It was to save the people he'd have gone on to kill in the village. The children most of all. I didn't much care back then what happened to me.'

Meg nodded. 'Did it make a difference, do you think?'

'For a while, yes, it did. The second in command called off the action and ordered us back to base. I doubt if he had much stomach for it either.'

'But the sergeant didn't die immediately, did he.'

'No. He seemed more or less okay when we began to carry him back to the base. But it was rough going and the bleeding was suddenly bad. The bullet must have nicked an artery.'

'You helped carry him, didn't you. How did you feel about that?'

'Only numb, I think. He asked me to give a message to his young son. As I told you, the kid would have been about nine or ten at the time. I didn't see his dad die. That happened back at the base.'

'What became of the message he gave you?'

'I told it to an officer at the base. He said he'd make sure it was passed on.'

'Did the sergeant say his son's name when he gave you the message?'

'I've thought about that. I don't remember. I don't even remember the message now. You retain some things when you're in shock but not everything.'

Meg decided that she wanted a drink now and said so. If anyone could do with a drink, Colin looked as if he could. She had no real opinion about it. She'd prefer it if he didn't order one for himself, but either way she wasn't going to comment. He headed for the bar, there was the usual wait and then he returned with red wine for her and a lemon squash for himself.

She looked up at him as he put the drinks on the table. 'So the son grew up and joined the army too?'

Colin sat down. 'I presume so. I'd been back here about ten years when the threats began. I changed my name and we moved a couple of times. Lucy hated that.'

'Did she know the true story?'

'Yes, or she would've insisted on me reporting it. Even got me into a military court or something. I knew I couldn't safely do that and she needed to know why. Telling her didn't help the way things were going between us.'

'I'm sure it didn't.'

'But the thing I'm wondering about now is if it could've been Williams who ordered those roses from the shop. It was a strangely out-of-the-way address.'

Meg took this in. 'That's very scary. Do you really think so?'

'No. I don't think anything because I don't know. And it's a long call. She's got that different surname and no clear connection to me. All I can really do now is make her harder to get to.'

'And she still doesn't know about this man?'

'No. But I may need to tell her so she'll take extra care. I couldn't have done that in the hospital with Lucy hanging around.'

'Would Lucy tell her?'

'I don't think so. When I told her back then, she saw some sense in what I'd done, or thought I'd done. The emotional sense anyway.'

'Do you think the officer's death saved the village?'

'If he'd survived, he would have ordered a rampage, and more than the baby and the old man would have died.' He drank some of his lemon squash and looked directly at her. 'What about you? Do you see any sense in what I...may have done?'

Meg thought about it. She answered slowly. 'Well, maybe. I guess I do.'

'And why I lied to you?'

She didn't respond.

He took a deep breath and asked the next question. 'So, what does this mean for us?'

She stared at him, not knowing what to say. What else could he be lying about? She knew he'd been exposed to terrible things during the war and she hadn't, but she had to be able to trust him. He was still watching her.

She said, 'I'm not sure. Not today, anyway.'

He reached out to her, but then took his hand away. He looked beaten and very sad. Meg felt that she couldn't give in to that, or not yet anyway.

'You can ask me anything you want,' he said.

'And will you give me a true answer?'

He didn't respond to that, and they got up, leaving their half-empty glasses, and walked past the other tables towards the door. Suzanne was at one of them with her friends and they seemed to be drinking fast. She looked up at Meg and gave her a nod but didn't smile. Meg nodded too, then turned away. She didn't need another hostile, dog-related encounter with the head of the strata committee on this particular night.

16

The river, the trees and the tiny explosions of fish jumping in the dark water had a calming effect on Meg as they walked back along the path. A woman was approaching out of the darkness with a small brown and white dog much like Bindi. They nodded to each other and the woman and the dog went on their way. A distant golf buggy started up. Why would you need a golf buggy at night, Meg wondered? But at least the ordinary world was going on and Bindi was at home, either waiting for her or asleep.

Colin stared out at the river. 'The water's inviting tonight, isn't it.'

She looked out at the shining pathway of moonlight on the surface. What he'd said was true, but something in his tone made Meg feel like it was more than a passing comment.

She glanced at him sidelong. 'Inviting in what sense?'

He didn't reply, but she understood what he'd meant.

'Is that the sort of thing you still think about?' she asked.

'Sometimes.' He paused. 'It would keep Beth safe.'

'But would affect her very badly.'

'Maybe, maybe not. And I'm sure, as a doctor, you've got your own tidy plans if it comes to that, haven't you?'

She could've lied about it but decided not to. 'Yes. Doctors have it easier, I guess. Pentobarbital is best. The vets use it to put down animals.'

'And you have it?'

She realised she'd in effect invited that question. 'If I did, I'd keep it well hidden.'

'Somewhere in your flat?'

She didn't answer.

He continued. 'So it's something you've thought about too?'

'I've been to dementia wards. I'd prefer not to be in one of them.'

'Do you have dementia in your family?'

'An aunt, yes, but it's not all that close. And it's a risk to both of us as we get older.'

They walked on along the dark path. There was something more she needed to ask him. 'Why did you choose the golf club to tell me the truth of what happened in Vietnam?'

'I wanted somewhere you could leave if you needed to, away from your place or mine.'

Meg wondered about this. It was true she could have walked out on him, walked home, but might she have done something similar herself in a wartime situation? He was a nasho who'd naturally seen things in a different way to the regular soldiers, and he'd only been there because of a random marble.

She still wasn't sure how things would go, but she felt certain of one thing. 'Whether or not you fired the shot that killed his father, we have to do something about this man.'

'We?'

'Yes, we. He's already had his revenge over the years since it happened. He needs to understand that people know who he is. And, if you come to any harm, the police will know too.'

Colin considered this. 'It's interesting you say that. I'd been thinking that maybe I should confront him. Settle it one way or another.'

'What, hand to hand combat? He's at least ten years younger than you.'

'I know.'

'It sounds more like you'd give him a chance to kill you, then dump your body in the river. I'm sure you wouldn't be the first dead man in that river in the last two hundred years.'

She looked at it again, calm and mysterious in the moonlight, and she thought about how many bodies might have gone into the water over the years. Maybe they'd been carried out to sea or maybe their bones were still there on the riverbed, perhaps rocked back and forth by the tide each day.

'Do you remember when it was called the River of Death in the newspapers?' Colin asked.

'My parents told me to keep away from it, but I don't remember why.'

'In the early seventies, it was nearly Christmas and there was an industrial spill of cyanide that flowed into the river from a creek. Cup and Saucer Creek was its name. All the fish were dead, and there were police on foot along the river to stop people swimming.'

'Did anyone die?'

'I don't remember.'

She tightened her jacket around her. It was getting colder. 'Have you told anyone else what's going on with this man? Anyone like a lawyer?'

'Yes, I have, and I keep in regular contact with him. If I disappear or if I'm found in the river, he'll send the details I've given him to the police.'

They were approaching the end of the path. Ahead of them was the open area where the helicopter had crashed.

She decided to ask the next question, awkward though it was. 'Did you tell your lawyer you did it? Or at least that you think you did?'

'No. Most lawyers don't want to know if their clients are guilty. It complicates things for them if they do. It's only you and Lucy. I'd had no direct contact with this man for a while, or at least not until the news crew gave me away. I haven't needed to tell anyone else.'

'I think we need to find out where this man lives. He's been operating in a kind of vacuum so far, believing you won't go to the police. If he's aware that other people know, and might report him, I think you're safer.'

They had reached the point where the path ended and there was overhead street lighting. He turned to look at her.

'Imagine if you had been pregnant. We'd have had a whole life together perhaps. Or perhaps I'd have already messed that up too.'

In some sense she agreed with him, but Meg couldn't say it out loud. Instead she answered, 'But then you wouldn't have Beth.'

'True. I wouldn't.'

They crossed the grass, which was wet from the rain showers and the falling dew. The lights weren't on in her flat, meaning that Nick wasn't there yet.

Colin stopped suddenly. 'Do we agree then? I'll hire a private detective to find out where he lives, or at least try to?'

Meg wasn't sure that involving a private detective was a good idea, but she didn't have anything else to suggest. 'Okay'.

'Whoever takes the job won't have much to go on other than his possible surname. It's something of a long shot, but I don't know how else to go about it.'

Meg didn't answer. When they reached the shared entrance to the flats, Colin kissed her lightly on her forehead, then turned away.

Meg felt tired and emptied out as she went down the black-carpeted corridor to her own flat. Beth's accident and how it happened was nagging at her. If it was Williams who'd forced someone entirely unconnected with the war off the road as part of his revenge, surely it was enough and he'd give it up now. But she couldn't convince herself that this was true. If the same man had done it, had proved himself capable of it, then the threat remained.

She took a book to bed, but questions continued to nag at her and kept her awake. Would there be a continuing stiffness and unease between her and Colin now that she knew he'd probably murdered someone? Would the long and peaceful evenings looking out at the trees from his back veranda still happen in the way they had so far? She finally put the book down and tried to sleep, but as she was drifting off she heard sounds of anger and frustration outside the door. Then somebody seemed to be crying. Meg's first thought was for Linh. Maybe she was having more trouble with Adrian. She put on her dressing gown and went out into the corridor.

Suzanne was sitting on the floor leaning against her own door and crying. She looked nothing like the fierce head of the strata committee, who was planning to evict Bindi. Meg glanced at her watch and saw it was almost one o'clock in the morning. Suzanne became aware of her and looked up blearily. Meg didn't much want to deal with whatever this was but felt she could hardly walk away.

'What happened?' she asked.

Suzanne was finding it hard to talk through her tears. 'I…don't have…'

'Your keys?'

Suzanne continued with a typical note of aggression. 'I'll sit here all night and in the morning I'll call a locksmith… except I can't because I'm due in court. My cat's in there too and I need to feed her and let her out.'

Suzanne's clothes were muddy, probably from a fall on the path back from the golf club. She tried to brush some of the mud off with the back of her hand, a clearly useless attempt. Meg hesitated. The night was mild and she could have left Suzanne in the corridor and slipped back into her own place.

Suzanne said, 'I'm sorry. I've… I've had a few tries with IVF and this one nearly worked. I lost it a couple of days ago, another one.' Her voice cracked.

'Do you have a partner? I mean someone I could call…?'

'I was doing it all on my own…' She corrected herself. 'With a donor. I'll be thirty-eight in a few weeks… You have a daughter, don't you?'

'No, I don't.' She didn't want to talk about her own loss with Suzanne. 'You can sleep on my couch if you like. My son won't be back tonight.'

She led the way into the flat and Suzanne headed with relief for the couch.

Meg stepped in quickly. 'Let me get some sheets before you lie down. You're quite…muddy. It's reasonably comfortable though. It's new.'

Bindi came out of Meg's bedroom and, as always, jumped up onto the couch.

Suzanne looked at her in vague surprise. 'The dog likes it too.'

'She does,' Meg said pointedly.

'And the owners' vote on her comes up soon.'

Meg removed Bindi from the couch and got out fresh sheets. 'You'd best get some rest.'

The reminder about the coming vote on Bindi troubled her. Other things had taken first place lately, but what could she do if the owners voted against her having a dog? Jonathan could probably drag it out for a while and make it annoying for the strata committee to pursue. Most of them wouldn't want to bother, but Suzanne, the lawyer, could run the case cheaply and wasn't likely to let it go.

She carried Bindi back to the bedroom, leaving the door partly open so Suzanne could call her if she needed to. Then at last she managed to sleep with the little dog beside her, but in the morning she woke to find Bindi gone. Puzzled and slightly alarmed, she put on her dressing gown and went to look for her. She found her sleeping on the couch beside Suzanne, who had an arm around her. Bindi woke and looked up at Meg.

'Sleeping with the enemy,' Meg whispered. 'Shameless.'

Bindi jumped down, waking Suzanne, who looked around in a daze. 'What time is it? I've got to be in court.'

'You can't go like that.'

'Like what?' Suzanne sat up. She had slept in her clothes and look down at them with a puzzled expression. 'That's a lot of mud, isn't it.'

'Yes, quite a lot.'

'And I still can't get into my place, can I?'

'No, but we're probably about the same size so you can wear some things of mine. They may be old-fashioned but courts are too.'

Suzanne didn't argue and some clothes were sorted out. She washed her face and cleaned her shoes while Meg made coffee and toast for breakfast. Suzanne said she'd call a locksmith from work and prepared to go.

'I'll leave your things outside your door later in the day,' Meg told her.

'And I'll return yours. Cleaned, professionally cleaned.'

It was clear that Suzanne found it embarrassing to be there and she left with unsmiling thanks.

Meg looked down at Bindi. 'It was a nice try, but I think she's still coming for you, little one. I've seen her type before.'

~

Colin had said he didn't want to burden her with the truth of what he'd done – or might have done – and that had been his reason for lying to her. But then he had told her the truth and, yes, she was finding it a burden. She'd started to call his number several times but had stopped before it went through. She needed to see him face to face.

During a second night of restless sleep, it occurred to her that Nick's contacts and connections with the dark web might somehow help to find the man who'd been threatening Colin. She'd heard Nick come in during the early hours of Sunday morning and knew he'd be asleep on the couch with Bindi beside him. She crept out to the kitchen, thinking she might at least make herself a coffee, but the little dog stirred when she saw Meg, then jumped down, waking Nick.

Over breakfast she told him, without any further detail, that there was a man with a motorbike who was stalking Colin, that his surname could be Williams and they needed to find him soon.

'What's the make of his motorbike?' Nick asked.

Meg was already irritated. 'What's that got to do with anything?'

'Do you know? Was it a Harley, a Triumph, a Yamaha?'

'I think Colin said it was a Triumph. Yes, I'm sure it was.'

'And this guy's been harassing him at home, has he? Like a lot?'

She answered impatiently. 'Yes. Yes, he has.'

'Then I think I've seen him.'

She stared at him. 'What? Where?'

'You know how the two streets intersect below Colin's place? How one goes on up past him and over the crest of the hill, and the other one weaves around and comes by us here?' She nodded and he went on. 'It was beginning to get dark and a guy was sitting on his motorbike at the intersection. It was like he was watching for someone. And, yeah, it was a Triumph. Red and silver on the petrol tank.'

Meg knew that a lot of motorbikes might have those colours, and in different makes, but it was chilling all the same. 'Did you see his face?'

'No, he had his helmet on. I was really just looking at the bike. It's a classic. But he must have thought I was watching him because he reached back and tried to cover the number plate with his hand. It seemed odd. That's why I remembered it. And it does say something, I think.'

'Yes, it does. It certainly does.'

'But there were like seven letters or numbers so he couldn't cover it completely. I saw two numbers, a five, a three and what looked like the letter K. I'm not sure about the K. It might've been something else. But maybe it's enough to work with.'

'How?'

'There's a service I can run it through. It's on the dark web. The cops use something like this if a witness can only give them a partial number plate. We should get a few possibilities. Williams is his name, is it?'

Meg nodded. 'As far as we know.'

'So do you think he lives somewhere near here? Or could he be out in the country? Do you know anything else about him? How old he might be?'

She thought about it. 'Since he's got a motorbike, he could be anywhere. But given the way he comes and goes, it feels to me like he's closer. Colin thinks he's probably in his late fifties, maybe sixties. Does that help?'

'It's all we've got.'

She took Bindi out for a walk while Nick worked on his laptop. They went towards the bridge and Meg looked to see if the pelican was in his place beneath it. He wasn't there. A bigger dog began to bark at Bindi in a threatening way. Meg picked her up, and they turned for home.

'That dog's like Suzanne,' she muttered to Bindi. 'I don't know how much I can do about her but I'll keep trying.'

She hadn't expected Nick to be finished when they got back but he already had a list of potential names.

He explained it to her. 'I tried it first with the two numbers I was sure of. But then it meant I had fifty-plus possibles with that surname...'

Meg was disappointed. 'Oh.'

'Some of them were either too young or too old or too far away. But then I ran it again with the K included, and with ages between late fifties and early sixties. That narrowed it down to five in this state. It seems like not many old guys ride motorbikes anymore.'

'That's because they're all dead.'

Nick gave her a half-smile. 'Not all of them. There's one in Wollongong, one in the Northern Beaches and another two in the western suburbs. All possible. But there's also one in the Inner West. Phillip Henry Williams, date of birth February 5, 1960. That makes him about sixty-two now.'

'Yes, it would.'

'But why would he do this, Mum?'

She didn't want to lie to Nick, but she couldn't tell him yet.

He continued, 'If he's going to all this trouble, I assume it's something big.'

'Yes. I suppose it must be.'

'There's nothing that tells us the make of the motorbike, but I've got addresses for the five of them and I saw that your car's back. We can drive by and see if any of them have a Triumph with a red and silver petrol tank. We should probably start with Phillip Henry.'

'But what do we do if we find the right one?'

'We're only looking for the motorbike. We don't need to get out of the car. And you can wear a disguise if you like?'

'This isn't a joke, Nick.'

'I'm serious. I'll wear a hat and sunnies. You can wear sunnies too and put a scarf over your head, like a movie.'

She looked across at him. 'All right.'

17

It took about half an hour to drive to the first house. It was on a quiet street with many parked cars along it and was close to Sydney Harbour. Church bells were ringing. The house was old and solid, built of brick and sandstone like others in the street, and it looked to Meg as if it was inherited from an older generation. There was a garage beside the house with a roll-down door and there were a few trees around it, along with several patches of grass that had not been mowed for a while. A tyre on a frayed rope hung from one of the trees. The house seemed closed up and silent, with heavy curtains over the windows.

She was disappointed. 'It looks like they're away.'

Nick agreed. 'We'll go round the block. If there's no sign of anyone we'll try the two out west.'

He drove them around the circuit. When they came back, a car was pulling out of a parking space in front of the house. Nick turned the wheel quickly and took the space.

Meg was beginning to get worried. 'Should we be this close?'

He looked at her in her concealing hat and sunglasses. 'Who are you? Have I met you before? Were you in a movie?'

She gave him a weak smile. She was beginning to think that a drive-by hadn't been a good idea. It was unlikely that any of the five would leave a vintage motorbike out where it could be stolen. Could they really go to each of the remaining doors and ask whoever lived there if they had one?

'Maybe we should tell the police what we've got,' she suggested, 'and they can take it further.'

'But Colin doesn't want to involve the cops, does he?'

Nick had figured that out correctly. Unsure what to do, Meg glanced back at the house and saw that the front door was opening. A man came out and headed towards the garage. She couldn't see enough of his face to judge his age but she thought he could be about sixty. He pointed a remote at the garage door and it began to rise slowly. The church bells continued to ring.

Nick was watching the man with amused surprise. 'So he's going to church, is he?'

'Not if he's…' She stopped.

'The one you want? He could be. Religions are all about revenge. An eye for an eye, remember?'

She was getting very nervous. 'I think we shouldn't stay parked here. It's too obvious.'

'No, wait…wait…'

The rising door revealed an expensive-looking black car but no motorbike.

She felt strangely relieved. 'He's only got a car. Let's go.'

Instead of starting the engine, Nick pressed the switch for the bonnet and began to get out of the driver's seat.

Meg was becoming really afraid. 'What are you doing?'

He didn't answer but went to the front of her car. He lifted the bonnet as if checking on the battery or the ignition. Then he came back in a leisurely way to the driver's seat.

'Bingo. It's there right at the back. A Triumph. Red and silver.'

Meg saw the man turn towards them as if he'd sensed he was being watched. 'He's looking at us. We need to go.'

'Then take a photo of him. Do it quick.'

Meg might have argued but there was no time. She reluctantly held up her phone to her window, took a photo, then slid further down in her seat.

She hissed at Nick. 'Go now! Go!'

He drove off slowly. Meg looked back, using her scarf to cover most of her face. She could see that the man hadn't gone into the garage but remained standing outside. He seemed to be watching them leave.

Nick glanced at her. 'You're really frightened of him, aren't you? Did you get the photo?'

Meg checked her phone. 'It's lopsided but fairly clear.'

She half-expected to hear the roar of a motorbike coming after them, but Nick took several sharp turns, doubled back, then took another. No-one was following. Meg stared down at the photo on her phone. The man's age was about right, she thought – in his early sixties. He still had his hair, which was grey and cut short, and the stiff, erect bearing of someone who'd spent much of his life in the army or the police force. He hadn't gained the weight you might expect at his age.

'Do we assume he's the one?' Nick asked her. 'Or do you still want to check on the others? I've got the rest of Sunday if you do.'

Meg knew that, when she finally reported all this to Colin, it'd be better if they hadn't just settled on the first man they'd seen. She'd left Bindi's fake-grass litterbox on the balcony, as well as food and water, so they could stay out. She looked again at the photo. Although he was at home on a Sunday morning, the man's clothes hadn't been sloppy. Dark grey pants and a light blue shirt. The tyre on the frayed rope had suggested grown-up children and maybe a wife still living with him. Having a family might make it easier to deal with him because he'd have more to lose. Though there could be no certainty that this was the right man, and it was unlikely that they'd found him first try, she felt that they might have done exactly that. She also rather liked the idea of spending Sunday driving around with Nick.

'Let's at least try the two in the western suburbs,' she said.

They found the next two men but they were easily eliminated. The first had put his motorbike, an old Yamaha, for sale out the front. The second had an open shed with a loosely-covered shape too small to be a Triumph. Meg wasn't sure if they should go on to Wollongong, but Nick said they might as well. It seemed to her that he was rather enjoying being out on a secret mission with his mother on an otherwise empty Sunday.

They had a fish-and-chip lunch on the Wollongong foreshore, then set off for the next possibility. They could see a motorbike in a shed out the back, but it had a cover

over it so they couldn't see the make. Nick went to the door on some pretext but was told that the owner had been away up north for the past six months. They drove finally to the Northern Beaches and saw an old Triumph in a parking space beside a block of flats. It wasn't covered and the petrol tank was black.

Meg looked round at her son. 'No?'

'No. I've got a clear mental picture of the one I saw. It was definitely red and silver. We can go back now, I think.'

It pleased her that they'd checked out them all. 'Thank you, Nick.'

'You're not ready to revisit the first one, are you? We could tell him we know who he is.'

She was startled by the idea. 'No, absolutely not. And I don't want you anywhere near him.'

'Whatever happened, it was a long time before I was born.'

'I'm not sure that would protect you. If Beth…' She stopped as she heard a text come in on her phone.

It was from Colin – *Am back in the mountains. Sorry I didn't let you know before. Beth released from hospital but needs two weeks physio. Will stay with her. Lucy going home. Have a private detective looking into our problem. No news yet. Sorry again but glad of this time with Beth.*

Okay, Meg thought, it is now 'our problem' and becoming more so day by day. Was he hoping that, given time, she'd get over the fact that he'd lied to her? She might be able to do that, but how much of Colin's life, she wondered, had been about avoiding things. Like giving up on university when someone handed him a leaflet.

It had been so different for Leon, who'd got his degree, then stuck to his business and built it up. But Leon's marble hadn't been drawn out of the barrel and Colin's had. Meg felt because of this that she should do what she could for him, even though they might already be drifting apart. It was for Beth as well.

There was a car in her space under the flats when they got back.

'You can complain to the strata committee,' Nick pointed out.

'Not while they're getting ready for the vote on Bindi.'

'You think they won't let her stay?'

'That woman down the corridor, the lawyer, clearly thinks the vote will go against us. It's as if she's trying to demonstrate the control she has over this place. People seem to be going along with her.'

'Because they don't want to get in a fight.'

'You think?'

'You can't blame them. Everyone lives so close together.'

'I do. I blame them. But most of all I blame her. How would she feel if I stole her cat and held it to ransom? Let Bindi stay or I'll drown it in the river.'

Nick looked startled. 'Would you do that?'

'I'd be tempted.'

He looked at her more closely. 'You seem tired, Mum. You go inside. I'll find a street park.'

'That's not so easy here. Not with all the Sunday golfers.'

'I know.'

Meg was glad to be welcomed by Bindi as she unlocked her door. She answered Colin's text with a message that said nothing about finding the man and the motorbike. It could wait until he got back. But at the same time she was beginning to think about making a move on her own. Jonathan had called to say he had two more things he wanted her to sign and she had a lunch appointment with him next day. Perhaps she'd ask his advice.

~

Flowers were coming out in gardens all the way as she set off in the late morning to walk there. More rain was forecast but so far the sky was clear. Jonathan was waiting for her in the same Vietnamese restaurant. She signed the forms that once again could easily have been posted to her and they ordered lunch.

'I've found a dog I like,' she told him, 'and I want to keep her. Her name's Bindi.'

She didn't explain that the dog had belonged to Nick. She didn't want to hear any more advice about her son.

Jonathan looked at her, puzzled. 'You mean you've acquired this dog already? Didn't you check the by-laws first?'

'I already knew what they might be.'

'Bindi? That's really her name?'

'Yes. And it might not be a matter of winning so much as dragging it out. There might even be grounds for launching a counteraction against the cats in the building. They make noise at night, they piss everywhere and there's always the risk to wildlife.'

Jonathan looked amused. 'How big is this dog?'

'She'd be about three kilos.'

'Barely a roast beef. Hardly threatening then.'

'I agree, but a lawyer on the strata committee's pursuing it.'

'Ah, yes. You've got to watch out for lawyers. They can have an autocratic tendency.'

Meg couldn't resist it. 'Are you talking about yourself?'

'Of course but, yes, all right, I can take on the dog and cat case if you want me to. At mate's rates. But I do point out that after only a few weeks in your new lodgings, you are already quarrelling with the neighbours.'

'Not all of them.' She knew she should come to the real point and tell him about the man threatening Colin. She was aware that she was shaking slightly. 'And there's something else. Something bigger.'

'Bigger than a roast beef? Really? Do go on.'

She did, and he listened without comment until she'd finished. She mentioned Beth's accident and that the police were still looking for the rider of the motorbike that had run her off the mountain road. As she'd expected, he asked no questions about whether Colin was guilty or innocent of the shooting while on patrol. She said her main fear now was that once Colin had an address for the man stalking him, he'd confront him on his own and might get himself badly injured or even killed.

'Has he talked to a lawyer about all this?' Jonathan asked.

'He's given details to his own lawyer in case something happens to him. It seems to me rather too late.'

'Can I ask something direct and personal?' Jonathan didn't wait for an answer. 'Are you in love with this man?'

'I would have married him once.'

'Before you met Leon?'

'No, the three of us were friends both at school and later on.'

'Then this man Colin, he went to Vietnam and Leon didn't?'

'Yes.' She'd said it flatly and in a way intended to head off any further questions along these lines. 'So what can I do? Colin's in the mountains now, but once he's got an address he'll want to act on it.'

'And you don't think that's safe.'

'No, I don't.' She paused for a breath. 'But I could do it.'

She'd half-expected Jonathan to argue against it, but he didn't.

'You could. But you need a witness, don't you, and you don't want to involve your son any further.'

She was emphatic. 'No, I don't.'

Jonathan considered it. 'I agree with the measure of confronting him. You let him know that there are other eyes on him and so you're effectively asking him how much gaol time he wants to do. The only trouble is that from tomorrow on, I'll be in court for the rest of the week and maybe longer. I also have commitments on the weekend.'

Meg took this in. 'What about this afternoon then?'

'Well…this afternoon's all right.'

It occurred to her that he might have left the time open after the lunch meeting. It was possible that he'd had something else in mind.

Jonathan clasped his hands, put his elbows on the table and leaned towards her. 'I feel the need to remind you of something, Meg. When I last saw you, you wanted a quiet life on your own and you were only worried about your son. This is suddenly much bigger than either him or Bindi the dog.'

'I know.'

'All right then, let's do it.' He got up. 'This man may not be there of course.'

'He might be.'

'Yes, he might. And there are always alternatives, like leaving a handwritten letter under his door as proof that we know where he lives.'

He got up to pay the bill at the counter.

Meg called after him. 'Let me share it.'

He paid and returned briskly. 'Next time. We'll take my car.'

They walked to his car which was in a small parking garage behind his building. Jonathan put the address into the GPS and they set out. Meg was a little dazed by the speed of it all, but relieved too. Whatever happened, they would be doing something against this man. It might even make a real difference.

'Colin won't like it though,' she told him, talking over the stilted, insistent voice of the woman on the GPS. 'He won't like me interfering this way. But whatever happens, I'll need to tell him afterwards.'

The road unrolled in front of them. They were getting closer every moment. She braced herself as a car cut in ahead.

'Would you really need to tell him?' Jonathan asked. 'As long as it stops, isn't that the point of it?'

'If it does stop, Colin would need to know rather than still waiting for an attack.'

'Yes, all right, I suppose so.'

'He might be angry enough not to want to see me again.'

'That would be a little unreasonable, I think.' Something occurred to him. 'Oh, but there's one thing. Say nothing about his daughter. If this man did cause the accident, he won't admit it. If he didn't, you may give him fresh ideas.'

Meg had already thought of this herself. 'Colin changed his name several times because of the threats. This man probably thinks of him as Peter Brown. We should keep it like that.'

They were winding through back streets. Meg thought he was driving too fast but didn't like to say anything. She was relieved when they pulled up safely outside the house and the woman's voice on the GPS told them they had arrived. Together they looked at the house, and Meg wasn't surprised to see that the roller door to the garage was down.

Jonathan insisted on going in alone first. 'I'll tell him you're out here and would like to speak to him. You've got your phone. Keep it ready.'

Meg was uneasy about this but it did make some sense. She didn't expect that the man, if he was there, would do anything to Jonathan. She watched him as he knocked on the front door and waited.

She'd begun to think no-one was there but then the door opened. Some words were exchanged with an unseen person and Jonathan went inside without hesitation. Meg couldn't think of anyone, apart from the police, who'd have gone straight into the house in the confident way that Jonathan had just done. Perhaps she'd underrated him in the past.

Time went by. Five minutes, ten, then fifteen. Meg began to wonder if something bad could have happened in there. She stared straight ahead thinking about what she might do if Jonathan didn't appear soon. She was shocked to realise that Phillip Williams was knocking on the window beside her. He was indicating that she should come into the house too.

She got slowly out of the car. 'My son knows where I am and has your address.' She showed him her phone with her finger on one of the buttons. 'If I simply press this, it will alert him and the police will immediately be called.'

'That's assuming something happens to you. It won't, so come and join us.'

'Why didn't my lawyer come out with you?'

'He's enjoying his coffee.'

She stared at him, not sure whether to believe this. 'Is your wife here?'

'No. She left. It has been almost seven years, and my two sons have moved away now too. They have their own lives. But the cat and I remain. You and the cat will get along, he likes doctors.'

She gave up on the questions and followed him into the house and to the front room. It was impressive, with thick carpet, high ceilings and antique furniture. Full-length curtains of deep blue satin were drawn against the sun. The room was tidy and uncluttered, as one might expect with a man trained in the army, but the smell of age and dust was strong. So was her impulse to open a window.

The man read her expression. 'Nothing's changed since my wife left.'

She didn't answer but looked at Jonathan, who was sitting in an armchair with a cup of coffee. He nodded to her but said nothing.

'Would you like a coffee too?' Williams asked.

She shook her head.

'Then sit down.'

She sat on an upright chair and so did he. Although her life experience as a doctor had inclined her to think she could handle such a meeting, she felt a kind of juddering fear.

There was a brief silence, then he spoke directly to her. 'I know from your lawyer why you're both here and he can fill you in on anything you may have missed. But let's go straight to the essentials, shall we?'

She muttered her answer. 'Yes.'

'The shot your…friend fired came after the action was over and the enemy had retreated into the jungle again. It was murder and it was witnessed.'

Anger was already rising in her. It made it easier to speak. 'What about the village on the mountain slope and the old man carrying a baby? Both shot by your father?'

'There was no village and no child. Look up any history of the war. The Americans burnt the villages and shot people trying to escape. We didn't.'

Meg looked at Jonathan. He shook his head faintly. Don't try to argue with him, he seemed to be saying. He was right, she thought. They were only there to let this man know there were more eyes on him.

He went on. 'Your friend…what do I call him? Peter Brown? Or has he changed his name again?'

Meg said nothing.

Williams continued. 'My father used to say that the nashos were a lot of trouble. They didn't have the training or discipline of men in the regular army.' He continued to look at Meg, holding her eyes. His voice was steady and reasonable. 'The lives of some good regular army men were lost trying to get the nashos out of trouble. Some were okay, but there were others like your Mr Brown who made up stories to cover what they'd done or hadn't done in Vietnam. More often than not it was what they hadn't done.' He paused for effect. 'But in Mr Brown's case, yes, it was different and he found it necessary to keep changing his name to cover his tracks. That must tell you something.'

Despite her anger, Meg found it very hard to answer the calm certainty of this man. 'There was no finding against him.'

'That's because they didn't *want* to find against him. There were more Birthday Ballots to come that would yield up more nashos. They didn't want to give these kids cause to fear the process. They didn't want to fuel more demonstrations. So it had to be inconclusive and it was… What else do you want to say to me?'

Meg managed to calm herself enough to answer him clearly. 'That I think you've indulged in an unchallenged and wrongly motivated revenge for, what, forty or so years?

But you need to know that it's no longer one-on-one. More of us are aware of who you are and are prepared to call in the police if you…do anything. That includes threatening messages in the letterbox or a noisy drive-by on your motorbike.'

'Though you and Nick did your own drive-by, didn't you?'

Mention of Nick scared her badly, and most of all that the man knew his name. But she still managed to speak calmly to Jonathan. 'I think we should go now, don't you?'

He got to his feet. 'Yes, I do. I think the point of our visit has been made.'

Meg and the man stood up too. Jonathan took something from a pocket that looked like a black pen. She realised it was a very small recorder.

He went on cheerfully. 'I apologise for not mentioning this during the earlier part of our conversation. It's just a habit of mine.' He put the recorder back carefully in an inside pocket.

Williams watched him, seemingly unmoved. 'What were you hoping for? Some kind of confession? But that's illegal anyway, recording me.'

'Is it? If anything happens to Mr Brown, there's enough here for the police.' Jonathan turned to Meg. 'Let's go.'

They let themselves out the front door and Jonathan shut it firmly behind them.

18

Meg's heart was beating fast as she got back into Jonathan's car. It was something of a surprise to her that ordinary suburban life was continuing around them – a mother with two young children, an old lady moving slowly on a walking frame, two tradesmen in yellow safety jackets on the footpath. She looked back at the house but the front door remained closed.

Jonathan glanced at her, then started the engine. 'I think…'

He stopped while he concentrated on pulling out of the parking space. 'We need a drink, or at least I do.'

Meg agreed and he drove them in silence to a pub near his office. He guided her through the noisy bar to a beer garden out the back. It didn't have much of a garden really – only a few pot plants spaced around – but it was quiet and peaceful and she was glad to sit there. The racing of her heart and the tingling in her nerve-ends was easing, and a sense of possible victory was growing. She'd done what she'd hoped to do. The warning had been delivered.

Phillip Williams could have said his father wasn't even in Vietnam and that might have been hard to disprove, but he hadn't done that. His name and address were known and there were witnesses. Anything harmful he now did to Colin would cause immediate suspicion and lead to investigation by the police. Jonathan's small recorder might have been illegal, but it could be useful all the same. She was glad that she hadn't tried to replace him as her lawyer. He had just done very well.

He went to the bar and brought back a whisky for himself and a red wine for her, then sat opposite her at the small table. They both breathed with something like relief for a few moments.

He raised his glass. 'Well. What did you think?'

Meg found that difficult to answer. Her feeling that they'd achieved something important was starting to drain away. She was feeling more puzzled than anything else by the visit.

'He seemed very calm and not even much concerned that we were there. It was as if he was expecting us.'

Jonathan shrugged. 'Well, yes, but men like that usually become calm, ice-cold, when they're under pressure in the witness box. That's how you can tell they're scared.'

Meg took this in. 'And I suppose you've encountered a few of them yourself.'

'I certainly have. And what it means is that there's nothing in him that you can appeal to, it's psychopathological. It's possibly not even out of love for his father that he's been doing these things. We don't know, but he believes Colin took something from him, and however long it takes him, this man will get his own back. He'd prefer not to go to gaol for murder of course, but men like this sometimes don't care.

And one thing he'll certainly do is to pride himself on avoiding scrutiny and not getting caught. And it's quite likely he could do that successfully.'

Meg absorbed this. Until now, she realised, the account of what this man had done and might do had seemed a little unreal to her. A little hard to believe. It was why she'd agreed to go with Jonathan to meet him. Yes, it was to tell him he was being watched, but it was also based on the hope that what was currently dark and festering might, if opened up to air and sunlight, more or less go away. But she also knew that the life and death aspects of war made it different in ways she could never know. It was in war that you could get used to the idea of killing someone on an eye-for-an-eye basis.

'There's a local parallel to this man,' Jonathan went on. 'You know about the Family Court bombings that happened years ago and the deaths that they caused? Also the bombing of the hall of the Jehovah's Witnesses? One man killed and about a hundred injured, including children? Another unsolved murder was linked to him but wasn't proved?'

'I know about him, yes.'

'He wanted both revenge and the custody of his daughter. For thirty years the police knew he'd done all these things but still they couldn't prove it. He went on being calm and open in police interviews. He always covered his tracks until the increased forensic capacity to investigate found him out. I suspect the man we just saw is a bit like that and, as a psychopath, he's an accomplished liar.' Jonathan was looking at her closely. 'Did he rattle you by the way he dismissed your friend's account? I mean, of the shooting of his father?'

She answered firmly. 'No.' But she knew it wasn't true. It had rattled her.

'There were several instances of an infantryman shooting a platoon commander on the Australian side, though I gather that in your friend's case nothing was concluded.'

'No, it wasn't.'

'And we were involved in a few cases of burnt villages, although we weren't like the Americans in that. I've read the histories.'

'But you weren't called up, were you?'

'I was, but at twenty I was in the middle of a law degree so I got out of it.'

'You were lucky.'

'I agree.' He looked at her seriously and went on. 'I doubt if there's any way to check further on what actually happened. Not at this distance and not if the army investigation at the time came to no conclusions. I think you may have to choose between this man's version and your friend's.'

Meg could see this too. Yes, she would have to choose.

Jonathan continued. 'And a shot supposedly fired after the action was over and in front of witnesses? It doesn't make much sense.' He thought for a moment. 'This man just added a little whipped cream, I think, to the chocolate pudding of his revenge by telling you that. To make you doubt...what shall I call him? Your friend? Your boyfriend?'

'I don't mind what you call him.' Meg looked at Jonathan steadily. 'And I don't doubt him.'

He nodded. 'I've seen men like this Phillip Williams before. And women too. I've even defended a few of them.'

'I suppose you would have.'

'And in the sense that they could stay perfectly calm under pressure and stick to their story whether true or not, then, yes, they were like him. The polite description now is sociopath, but psychopath is more accurate and descriptive and should stay. Certainly for him anyway. I suppose you had some of them come through your practice too?'

'Threats are not new to me, Jonathan.'

'I suppose not.' He looked at her. 'Are you in love with this man? I mean with…what's his real name again? Colin?'

Meg decided to be honest. 'I think so. I was once.'

'Then do you think your own life may be in danger too?'

'Possibly.'

'Your will, your estate all goes to your son, doesn't it?'

Meg was puzzled. 'Why are you asking that now? You wrote it.'

'And you haven't changed it since?'

She shook her head. 'Stop this, Jonathan.'

'All right. The time's getting on so I think we should go.'

They walked out to the street together through the cheerfully noisy bar.

'Did you drive up to see me or did you walk?' Jonathan asked as they approached his car.

'Walked.'

'I'll drop you home then, and although I think the man's had a stern warning…' He paused. 'I don't mean to scare you, but take care.'

'I will... He mentioned Nick's name. That frightened me.'

'It sounds like he may have been watching you too then.'

She shivered. 'It's creepy.'

'But other than taking out a Restraining Order...'

'Would you advise that?'

'Not really, Restraining Orders don't make much of a difference to men like him. And he'd probably fight it and drag it out for the fun of it. He'd also want to stay on your mind.' He unlocked his car and they got in. Jonathan looked across at her. 'You know I'm very fond of you, Meg.'

She couldn't find a way to answer this so she just smiled at him uneasily. He dropped her at the flats and she thanked him for the day, reminding him to send her a bill.

'This one's on the house,' he told her and drove off quickly.

Meg walked inside feeling that she had offended him, but at the same time she couldn't contemplate any kind of affair with Jonathan. He surely wouldn't expect it now that he knew about her feelings for Colin.

She looked around at the flat. A few things of Nick's were scattered about and the place already had something of a run-down feeling. She couldn't face doing anything about it and went straight to her bedroom with Bindi following happily. She lay down and let herself fall into a light sleep with the comforting warmth of the little dog beside her. It was late in the afternoon when she was woken by the sound of a key in the lock.

She called out in some fear. 'Nick?'

He came to the door of her bedroom. 'Who else?'

'No-one else.'

She got up, went into the main room and sat down heavily in the armchair while he took a corner of the couch.

'What did you do today?' he asked curiously.

It was hard to hide things from Nick. 'Jonathan and I went to see the motorbike man.'

'I thought you might do that.'

'Did you?'

'Yeah, once you had his address.'

She gave him a brief rundown of what had happened, leaving out the man's assertion that there had never been a village or an old man with a baby.

Nick looked at her thoughtfully. 'It was brave of you to go there, but you shouldn't try to deal with psychos, Mum. They're good at what they do. I've had dealings with a few.'

'In your dark-web life?'

'Maybe, but listen, I know Colin's kind of in love with you again. If he's telling you to stay away, then you should.'

'Is there really such a thing as being kind of in love?'

'I dunno. You're the grown-up.'

'And I'm grown-up enough to know I don't want to see Colin killed.'

'Let me think about it…'

She felt a sudden anxiety. 'But don't do anything yourself. The man knows your name. I think he may also know that you came with me to check out his place.'

'How would he figure that out?'

'I've no idea, but I don't like it.'

He nodded. 'We shouldn't leave the keys outside anymore. I'll get one cut for myself and give you back the spare. There's a chain for the front door. We should start using it.'

'Yes, we should.' She thought for a moment. 'I notice that the car in my space has gone. I'll move mine back now.'

'Would you like me to do that?'

She could see out the window that the sun was going down over the river in a blaze of red and gold. She felt like a walk after all they'd talked about.

'No, I can.'

~

She walked up to where Nick had parked her car on a section of the road above Colin's place. The engine coughed a few times when she started it, then seemed all right. Residents and golfers were parked on both sides of the narrow street so she drove over the crest of the hill and down to the turning circle. The engine cut out, and although her foot was almost to the floor, the car wasn't stopping. The brakes seemed to engage but not fully. It went over a low gutter and onto mud and wet grass and began to slide down the steep slope towards the river.

Meg tried to force the gear shift, but it wouldn't move. She accidentally bumped the driver's door latch. The doors all locked and the horn began to sound loudly and repeatedly. She felt a strange calm. If the car went into the river with the engine off, the windows wouldn't open. She'd be trapped. She must get out. She tried to undo her seatbelt but the pressure of her body against the clasp made it difficult. As the car continued towards the river, she managed to undo it.

She unlocked the driver's door and the horn stopped. She tried to throw herself out onto the grass, but the ankle strap on her left sandal caught, and she couldn't get out. She struggled to reach the strap, feeling panic. Then, with strength that surprised her, she tore the leather strap from the sole and launched herself out onto the muddy ground.

Then Nick was suddenly beside her. 'Are you all right?'

She nodded but couldn't speak. The car was moving slower now, heading for a tree near the river's edge. Nick ran after it. He managed to lean into the open door, and the car stopped.

He returned to crouch beside Meg. 'Are you sure you're all right?'

'I think so.'

He wasn't convinced. 'You might have concussion.'

'I didn't really hit my head. My shoulder took most of it... What are you doing here?'

He sat down beside her. 'I recognised the horn. I followed the sound and there you were. Driving illegally on the golf course.'

'I suppose I was.'

Nick retrieved her shoe from the car and he helped her stand up. She felt dizzy but otherwise not badly hurt. Every muscle was strained and she knew she'd feel it when the shock wore off, but it didn't feel like anything was broken. The sun was low over the river and she found the warm light strangely beautiful. She'd have liked to watch the last of the sunset with Nick, but she became aware of two men standing beside a golf buggy nearby. The younger man helped the older one back into the golf buggy, then came over to Meg.

His expression was grim. 'You nearly ran over us!'

'I'm sorry. I didn't see you.'

'Driving with your eyes shut, were you?'

'No, I was trying to control the car but the brakes didn't…' She couldn't go on.

The older man called from the golf buggy. 'At least she avoided the greens.'

Meg laughed as she turned away and set off unsteadily for the flats with Nick's support.

He was still worried. 'Are you sure you're okay to walk?'

'I'll have to be.'

Nick was looking back at the car. 'You ended up near where the chopper came down.'

She thought about it. 'A lot seems to have happened since then.'

'It has.'

Suzanne came to meet them as they approached the flats. 'Was that really your car out on the golf course? How did it happen? Are you all right?'

Meg only nodded, although in fact she was feeling increasingly shaken and off-balance.

'Good.' Suzanne spoke as if it was all over. 'I need to talk to you about the vote…'

Nick interrupted. 'Now is not a good time, okay?'

'Of course.' They moved on and she called after Meg. 'We'll talk sometime soon. You need to prepare yourself.'

Meg turned back. 'What? For a bad outcome?'

Nick shook his head fiercely at Suzanne.

She backed off. 'When you're better...'

Meg could feel her watching them as they moved on.

Once safely in the flat, Nick helped Meg to lie down on the couch, then got a blanket and put it over her.

'Keep warm, okay? I'll make you a hot drink. With sugar. Tea? Coffee?'

'Coffee, I guess.'

He went to make it. Bindi didn't follow but stayed on the floor beside Meg. She reached down and stroked the little dog's head to reassure her. He got the dinner ready and she ate a little, then he helped her to bed.

'Do you need something to get you to sleep?' he asked.

'Maybe. If you haven't sold it.'

He laughed. 'Not lately. I got the impression you didn't like that.'

She slept quite deeply, feeling safe with Nick on the couch and with Bindi, who would bark at any intrusion, beside her on the bed. When she woke up, she could feel the strain of what had happened in every part of her body. She had a shower and got dressed in her usual blue jeans and a shirt and jacket. Despite the pain and stiffening in her limbs, she felt rested, clear in the head and unexpectedly calm. She went to the kitchen and sat down at the small table while Nick made breakfast for them both.

She asked him the question that both scared and puzzled her. 'Was that just an ordinary accident, do you think? Or was it set up?'

'You can ask the cops to go over the car…'

'Should I do that?'

'Probably you should. But then you'll have to start naming names. Phillip Williams for a start.'

Meg shook her head. 'I need to wait till Colin's back. I haven't even told him about us having seen Phillip. I really don't want to do it over the phone.'

She sipped her coffee, feeling glad to be there in the kitchen with Nick and Bindi and still alive.

He sat down at the table. 'But about your car, you don't need the cops yet. If the brake cables were cut, that'd be clear to a mechanic.'

'But I'm not sure they were. My foot was close to the floor, but the brakes did grip a bit. You know how steep that slope is. Along with the weight of it and the wet and muddy grass, the car was just sliding down.'

'And we know you need knew brake pads.'

'We do. Okay, let's not guess anymore. We'll get it towed to Dimitri to check out.'

Dimitri came from a large Greek family and had looked after cars for Meg and Leon for many years. She knew he'd do the job well and not ask awkward questions.

Nick agreed. 'Fine. I'll also tell him it's just been in an accident on the motorway. That could make a difference.'

'It could.'

'There won't be fingerprints. If the guy did anything to your car, he'd have used gloves. But if Dimitri thinks something was done, then you'll have to tell Colin and call the police. I don't suppose you taped your meeting with the guy.'

'Jonathan did.'

'Good. I'll follow the tow truck on my motorbike and talk to Dimitri. You're not going anywhere.'

'What about the scaffolding?'

'Nothing's happening today, and I'm beginning to think you were right about it. I sometimes look down at the ground and it seems a very long way away.'

This alarmed her. 'Does it?'

'I'll probably get used to it…'

She interrupted. 'You don't have to do it. I can afford avocados for us both.'

He laughed and looked relieved, then he booked a tow truck and went out to wait for it. Meg took a painkiller for her shoulder and retreated to the couch. She would drift off to sleep but then she'd suddenly be alert again. After a while she heard a motorbike and reacted with alarm, but it was only Nick returning.

He looked troubled. 'Dimitri says the brake pads were very low. You knew that. But there's something else.'

'What?'

'The cables weren't cut…'

'Good.'

'What's not good is the brake fluid. It'd almost completely drained out.'

'So what does that mean?'

'He doesn't know. He says he can't tell if it was done deliberately or if the accident caused a leak.'

'But wouldn't the panel beaters have noticed that?'

'Not necessarily, and it's an old car. You may not like this, Mum, but Dimitri said you should switch to Dad's car. It's in much better shape.'

She thought again of how the car smelled and how it had reminded her of Leon. She could have it cleaned, but so much had been happening lately that she hadn't thought about it.

Nick continued. 'If you really don't want to use it, at least get a new hatchback and send yours to the wreckers. You shouldn't be sentimental about cars.'

'Or motorbikes?'

'Motorbikes are different.'

She smiled at him. 'That's the kind of thing your dad might say. You're like him.'

Nick didn't respond, but somehow he seemed taller. It was like he was taking up more space in the room. And, yes, it was true. He was like his dad, and if he was glad of it, then so was she.

19

Late in the afternoon, Meg heard a child crying, screaming really. It sounded to her like Teo. She opened the door and saw him running down the carpeted corridor. Nick came out, and together they brought him into her flat and set him down on the couch with Bindi beside him.

Meg sat down with him too. 'What is it, Teo?' she asked gently.

He could barely speak. 'Mummy, Mummy... Daddy...'

Nick looked across at her. 'I don't like the sound of that.'

She got up. 'I don't either. I'll go and look.'

He put out a hand to stop her. 'If his dad's around, I need to come with you.'

'We can't leave Teo here on his own.' She thought of something. 'I'll see if Suzanne's home.'

She was, and Meg told her firmly that she was needed to look after Teo. She was to keep the door locked and the chain on and not open it to anyone unless she was sure who it was, and especially not Teo's father.

Surprisingly, Suzanne didn't ask questions but came in and sat down on the couch with Teo and Bindi. Meg grabbed her medical bag, then she and Nick hurried down the corridor towards Linh's flat. Adrian was standing in the open doorway.

'The Iceman,' Nick muttered. 'Leave him to me.'

Adrian put his arm across the door to block them. 'This is my flat. You can't come in here without my permission.'

Nick responded casually and as if things were normal. 'Is Linh here? She and my mum are friends, you know.'

'She's not here.' Adrian hesitated. 'She went out to buy something.'

Meg knew he was lying. Linh would never have left Teo there alone with him.

Nick continued in the same mild tone. 'No problem. We can wait. But as you know, my mum's a doctor and she'd like to see inside.'

'Why?' Adrian demanded.

'Just to make sure things are okay. You know my mum. You met her at the park.'

Adrian didn't answer but continued to block the doorway. He was wearing black clothes, was taller than Nick and looked strong and dangerous. Meg waited anxiously, counting the seconds.

Adrian dropped his arm and took a few steps into the corridor. 'Where's Teo?'

She didn't answer but dodged around him and went into the flat. Linh was lying on the wooden floor. She seemed to be unconscious.

Meg knelt beside her. 'Linh? Can you hear me?'

Linh didn't respond. Meg pressed her fingers to her neck to check her pulse, then listened to her chest. Her breathing was steady but shallow. Meg ran her hands over Linh's head and neck. She found a sticky patch of hair at the back of her head but it wasn't a major bleed. She scooped her finger through Linh's mouth to check the position of her tongue, then used a couch cushion to stabilise her neck before she rolled her onto her side. She could hear Adrian talking to Nick in the corridor.

There was some fear in his voice. 'It's not like I did anything. She had a few drinks, that's all.'

'Enough to pass out?'

He didn't answer that.

Once Linh was resting on her side, Meg wiped her hand on her jeans and dialled triple zero. 'Ambulance… I'm a doctor. It's a young woman… A domestic incident, yes… She's unconscious. Airway is clear but her breathing's shallow. We need an ambulance immediately. The injury is consistent with an assault so…' She dropped her voice, hoping Adrian couldn't hear. 'Send police too.' She gave the address. The operator stayed on the line and soon told her the ambulance and the police were on their way.

Linh's body shook once, then she kicked both her legs out and rolled off the cushion onto her back. She exhaled and then her breathing stopped. Meg gripped her chin to open her airway, pressed her lips against Linh's and tasted blood. She blew two solid puffs of air and started chest compressions, counting aloud. 'One, two, three, four…' She kept going but could feel herself fatiguing after only two cycles. She might soon have to call Nick to take over.

'Please, Linh, don't do this.' Her voice was tight. 'Teo needs you.'

It was almost as if Linh had heard her. She coughed and began to breathe on her own again. Meg pressed the cushion to Linh's head and rolled her onto her side. She continued to check her pulse and breathing while hearing the voices from the corridor. Adrian kept saying loudly the flat was in his name and that he shouldn't be sleeping in his car while 'that bitch' lived here with his son. He told Nick that he'd got a lawyer and he was going to the Family Court. Teo should be living with him in the flat, not her.

Nick answered in mild tones. 'Yes, I understand… I'm sure this kind of thing feels really unfair… I can see your problem…'

It felt like a long time to Meg, but she knew it was only about seven or eight minutes before she heard the ambulance approaching. Two male paramedics came in and quickly began their assessment. She briefed them and added that, when Linh woke up, she'd need to know that Meg had her son, that he was safe and she would bring him to the hospital as soon as she could.

'Got it,' said one of them.

They fitted blocks on each side of Linh's head, then they carried her out on a spinal board and soon the siren started up again. Meg took her medical bag and went out to the corridor.

Nick was waiting there alone. 'Is she all right?'

'No, but I think she will be.' She added in a mildly acid tone, 'You were very nice to him.'

Nick made a sound of disgust. 'He's a scumbag. He was off his face on ice. If he'd thought I was challenging him, he'd have smashed me out of the way and come for you and Linh. He took off when he heard the sirens. But these guys are crazy strong when they're like that. You can't even get to them with a taser. Sometimes only a bullet will stop them. The cops are looking for him now.'

She put her arm round Nick. 'You did absolutely the right thing.'

'Let's go home.' He sounded exhausted too.

Suzanne undid the chain and opened the door for them. The setting sun was lighting up the flat as Meg got Teo something to eat and Suzanne finished her own version of the three bears. Meg knew that Suzanne would want to ask questions, but she seemed to understand that she shouldn't ask in front of Teo. She left, and Nick made up a little nest of blankets and pillows on the floor for Teo and Bindi. The little boy and the dog went almost instantly to sleep. Nick made sure the door was locked, then latched the chain.

Meg let some time pass before she phoned the hospital. She was told that Linh was recovering and her parents were there. Meg lay down on her bed and, despite the pain in her shoulder and her strained muscles, she was able to sleep.

Around midnight she was woken by someone knocking repeatedly on the front door, and she went out into the main room. Nick, awake too, signalled to her to let him deal with it. He went to the door but didn't open it.

'Who is it?' he called. The knocking stopped and there was silence. 'Who is it?'

After a pause they heard Adrian's voice. 'I need to collect my son.'

'We don't have him here, mate. Sorry.'

'Yes, you do. I've been watching and he hasn't come out. Let me talk to your mother.'

'She's not here either.'

'Liar!' He started kicking the door.

Meg checked on Teo, who was still asleep with Bindi in the nest of blankets. She thought the noise might wake him but he slept on.

Nick called out again. 'I wouldn't do that, mate. I've called the cops and they know where you are now.'

'Fuck you.'

Adrian kicked the door for a few more minutes. There was silence for a little while, then it sounded as if he was crying.

Meg expected the sound of police sirens, but they didn't come.

Nick turned away. 'Poor bugger. Sad, sad, sad.'

'Yes,' Meg agreed. 'Very sad.'

She went back to bed but lay awake for the rest of the night. In the morning she made Teo some breakfast, then called a cab, one with a child seat. She told Teo they were going to the hospital to see his mum.

'Can Bindi come too?' he asked.

'She isn't allowed to ride in a taxi.'

'Why not?'

'Because she's a dog. But Nick will stay here to play with her.'

~

Meg and Teo reached the hospital. Linh's parents were standing beside the bed. Linh was weak and pale, but when she saw Teo, she wrapped her arms around him and repeatedly kissed the top of his head. Then her parents led him away to buy an ice cream. They seemed gentler and more caring of Linh than Meg might have imagined.

Linh looked exhausted but she spoke clearly to Meg. 'He said that he'd come to evict me from his flat – *his* flat, though I pay the rent. He wanted me to go, but for Teo to stay there with him.' She shook her head at the impossibility of this. 'Then he went into the bedroom to look for the lease papers. I told Teo to run away as fast as he could and find you or someone in the flats to take him in. I could hear voices and I knew he'd found you. Adrian came back into the room, and when he saw Teo was gone, he grabbed me by my shoulders and smashed me backwards into the wall… You know the rest.'

'I do. And it was Suzanne who stayed with Teo while Nick and I sorted things out.'

'Her?'

'Yes, she was fine. I think she liked being with him and Bindi.'

Linh seemed doubtful. 'What happens now?'

'The police will come and talk to you. They may arrest Adrian again.'

She nodded. 'I have to move out of the flat. But my parents seem to like the idea of their grandson living with them.'

'And you too?'

'It's better than this.' She was silent for a moment. 'They told me I died for a few seconds.'

'You stopped breathing, yes. I was with you though.'

Linh was about to say more but her parents were returning with Teo. The little boy climbed into the bed with her.

She looked up at Meg. 'Thank you.'

'I'm glad I could help. You can bring Teo back to see Bindi. That's if I'm allowed to keep her.'

She wrote down her phone number for Linh and left.

On the way out she asked at the nurse's station about the boy and his uncle, the pilot, saying she was a GP who'd attended to them when they were still in the crashed helicopter. One of the nurses made some internal calls and found that the boy was home, though having some out-patient treatment. The pilot was still in hospital but was now able to do rehab.

'Did you want to see him?' the nurse asked.

Meg shook her head. 'He wasn't conscious when I was with him so it wouldn't mean much to him. He probably wouldn't want to be reminded of that night anyway.'

'The boy told one of the nurses that a nice lady stayed with him in the helicopter when it was nearly sliding into the river. Was that you?'

Meg laughed. 'I guess it was.'

She thanked the nurses and left.

She returned to her flat and was in the kitchen with Nick when she got a text from Colin. It said that he was coming back on the train and that the private investigator had found the address he'd been looking for. He wanted to know if they could meet. She showed the text to Nick.

'Are you worried?' he asked. 'You look it.'

'I don't know how he'll react to what we did in going to see the man. To what *I* did.'

'I'll keep out of the way if you like.'

'No, I'll meet him somewhere else.'

She texted Colin to suggest they meet at the golf club at midday. The rest of the morning passed slowly, and Meg kept checking her watch until it was finally twenty to twelve. She set out along the river path. More rain had fallen overnight and the water was high, covering the roots of the mangroves. The path was still wet and several small creeks trickled across it. Her shoes were wet too by the time she walked into the bar at the golf club.

There were a few people in the bar already. She ordered a coffee and found a small table as far from them as possible. Colin arrived a few minutes later. He seemed to her more focused and determined than he'd been in recent weeks. He told her straightaway that the private investigator had found Phillip Williams' address. He was now working out where and how he should confront him. Meg found all this dismaying. She'd been hoping that, even if Colin had hired a private detective, nothing would have been uncovered yet. Playing for time, she asked what the address was. He told her and it was correct. After that she could see no way out.

She answered as lightly and offhandedly as she could. 'The address is right. I've been there twice. First to check the place out and then to talk to him.'

'You *what?*' Colin stared at her. 'You're not saying you went there on your own, are you?'

'No, no, of course not. I went with Jonathan. He's the lawyer I told you about. He and I talked about the problem over lunch…'

'Oh yes?'

The grimness in his voice bothered her, but she went on. 'He offered to come with me. He said he could only do it that afternoon because of a long case coming up in court.'

'And you went?'

She answered more sharply. 'Yes, I went, and do you know why? I wanted to do something before that man does. Not depending on your lawyer to do it after…' She stopped.

He clasped his hands and leaned his elbows on the table, looking at her hard. She remembered Jonathan doing that once. 'But you've put yourself in real danger!'

She couldn't answer this and decided not to try.

He went on. 'Can't you see that going after you or Beth is the best way to get to me? Killing me would just finish it. He doesn't necessarily want that.'

'I know.'

'Do you know it? Really?'

'You saved me from the rotor blade. Without you, I'd be dead already.'

He wasn't persuaded. 'But this is harder and more complicated. Much harder.'

She sat back and looked at him. 'And you feel I'm interfering in your life, don't you.'

'Yes. But now I know where he lives...'

He seemed to be about to leave. Meg, alarmed, reached out and covered one of his hands, holding it down on the table.

'Don't go on your own,' she told him as forcefully as she could. 'Just don't do it.'

He freed his hand and pushed back his chair, about to stand. It grated loudly on the floor and people at other tables, who'd already heard the angry tones, turned to look. Meg became aware of a waiter who was watching them. Colin didn't stand up. He looked at her for a long moment as if thinking it all through, then pulled his chair back closer to the table. She braced herself for what he would say.

His voice was still hard. 'Since he knows about you, and maybe about Beth, I do need to deal with him. Deal with him now.'

Meg knew that her chances of persuading him not to see Phillip Williams on his own were lessening all the time. She had another thought. Nick could go with him – he knew the address – but she didn't say it. She couldn't risk that.

Instead she told Colin, 'Nick got me to take a photo of him on my phone. The first time.'

'Oh Jesus. Can I see it?'

She pulled her phone out of her handbag. 'That's him. He's big, and fit too, I'd say.'

'And so you met him, did you?'

'I did. And he seemed to me calm and dangerous. But he has a good house and something of a life, and now he knows that more people are watching him.'

Colin shook his head. 'Do you remember I called you a stupid woman once?'

'Yes.'

'And I love you and I hate you a little bit too. Is that okay?'

'It'll do.'

He got up and seemed about to walk off on his own. Meg knew suddenly that she shouldn't let him leave like this.

She stood up. 'I'll walk back with you. We needn't talk about anything.'

He looked at her closely to make sure she meant it. 'Okay.'

~

They said almost nothing to each other as they walked back along the river path. She thought she should possibly warn Colin about some of the things that Williams had said, but she decided that would have to wait. As they walked on, it seemed to Meg to be becoming a more companionable silence. It lasted until they reached the end of the path and the expanse of the golf course opened up in front of them. Colin stopped as if he had something to say. She stopped too and waited, fearing what it might be.

He turned to look at her and all he said was, 'I've missed you.'

She looked back at him. 'I've missed you too. Can't this stuff just be over?'

'Soon.'

Her car was already gone so she wouldn't have to explain to him what it was doing on the golf course. A dozen or so white ibises were foraging for curl grubs in the exposed earth. A few more were flying in. Meg could see the two men whose lives she had allegedly imperilled. They were inspecting the damage to the hillside with another man, probably a greenkeeper. She looked away but the younger man recognised her.

He called out, 'Returning to the scene of the crime, are you, madam?'

Colin frowned. 'What's he talking about?'

She tried to walk on. 'Ignore him.'

The man raised his voice after her. 'All this will take a lot of work to repair, you know. We may need to send you a bill for your insurance company. You're in the apartments over there, aren't you?'

'Yes, number one.'

'Let's hope the insurance company reacts favourably.'

She shrugged and walked on quickly.

Colin came after her. 'What aren't you telling me now?'

'I hadn't got around to it.'

'I think you'd better get around to it.'

She stopped and faced him. 'Come back to my place for a coffee. Nick might be there but…'

She walked on without saying any more. She couldn't hear him coming after her, but she didn't look back. There was a pause, and then she knew he was following.

Nick made coffee for the three of them and helped Meg explain more to Colin about what had happened. About her car and the loss of brake fluid and how their mechanic couldn't say whether it was accidental or not. Nick was quiet and steady and she was glad to have him there.

Colin absorbed it all. 'Since I'm planning to see the guy, I can ask him about the brake fluid.'

Nick shook his head. 'Whether or not he did anything to the car, he'll give you the impression he did.'

Colin took this in. 'True.'

Meg was relieved that he now seemed to be working out the elements of the problem, not just rushing ahead. She was pleased too by the way he talked to Nick as if he had a natural part in the discussion and had opinions worth listening to.

'Have the police told you any more about Beth's accident?' she asked.

Colin shook his head. 'No. Or at least she hasn't heard from them. But the two people closest to me have both had accidents that might well have been fatal. Accidents where nothing could be proved. That's quite a coincidence.'

'I'll give you that,' Meg agreed.

Colin looked at them both. 'So what now?'

There was a silence, then Nick spoke first. 'I don't think you should go to his house on your own,' he said to Colin.

'There's only one effective thing you can say – that more people are watching him. Mum and her lawyer have already done that. But, if you're determined to go, I'll go with you…' He saw Meg's expression. 'Though it might freak Mum out a bit.'

She summoned all the parental authority she could. 'You're not going, Nick!'

There was another silence. Nick broke it again. 'I know it may sound a bit piss-weak,' he said to Colin, 'but you could write him a letter. Threaten him with the cops and legal action if he does anything more.'

This appealed to Meg. 'And it would probably come best from Jonathan since he went with me to the house and he taped what was said. He'd write a good warning letter.'

Colin didn't respond.

'You're not convinced?' she asked.

'I'll think about it.'

Nick looked at him hard. 'Could you do one thing for us? Tell us if you're going anywhere near this guy? Mum won't stop worrying otherwise.'

Colin nodded. 'Okay.' He looked at Meg. 'But we all know he's not going away, don't we?'

There was a silence. Neither she nor Nick could argue with that. She asked Colin instead, 'How's Beth doing?'

'She's not over what happened to her but her physio's helping,' he told them. 'She doesn't want to leave the share house, so I'm getting cameras and alarms set up around it.' He got up to leave. 'I'll go back now into my own security-protected bunker. I need to settle for a while and think.'

He looked at Meg. 'And I suspect Nick will agree that you shouldn't stay over at my place for the time being.'

'What about daytime?'

He hesitated. 'I guess you could come for breakfast if you want to.'

'If it's all peaceful, yes, why not?'

Colin glanced at Nick. 'Okay with you?'

He nodded. 'You can't live in fear forever.'

'Can't you?' There was another brief silence, then Colin went on. 'But one strange thing about this man, I've never seen his face, except in that photo.'

'Then let's hope you don't see it.' Meg looked at him. 'I'll come for breakfast. Eight o'clock suit you?'

He nodded. 'I'll have the coffee ready.'

20

The morning was fresh and cool as Meg set out to walk up to Colin's house. Spring showers were forecast for later in the day, but so far the sky was clear. She saw an eagle being chased by a small angry bird, both of them flying all the way across the vast blue sky. She smiled to herself, feeling a kind of identity with the little bird and its foolhardy bravery.

She and Colin had a quiet breakfast together on the back veranda, looking out at the trees and hearing the magpies calling to each other. It seemed to Meg that Colin, having slept on it, had finally understood her purpose in going to see Phillip Williams. Once breakfast was done, they looked at each other. It was clear they were sharing the same thought.

'Is it too early to go to bed?' Meg asked.

'I don't see why.'

'Good.'

They spent a pleasant morning in bed that helped to re-establish what had been between them. It was approaching lunchtime when she commented that he'd been through a lot lately and that next time she came over for breakfast, she'd bring her medical bag. She'd check him out on the basics of blood pressure and so on.

'Okay. And when are you next coming for breakfast?'

'Tomorrow?'

'That'll do.'

'But I'll go now, I think.'

He nodded. 'And I need to work on ways to protect Beth. She still doesn't know why I'm doing this and she thinks I've gone crazy…'

'But you don't want to tell her why?'

'Not yet, though I may have to soon.'

'She'll deal with it, won't she?'

'Yes, I think Beth can deal with most things. Someone told me once she was an old soul.'

Meg walked home feeling that there might possibly be a consensus that would lead to some kind of order and control. She spent the rest of the day doing the things she'd planned. Surprisingly, Leon's car started and she drove it to Dimitri for cleaning and checking. She'd decide later what to do with it.

The following morning, she and Colin sat together over coffee on his back veranda. The day was warm and almost still, and Meg looked now and then into the wide blue sky for the eagle and his tiny pursuer. It seemed as if the small bird might have driven his enemy away.

Colin's phone rang and he looked down at the screen. 'It's Beth.'

He walked out into the back garden to talk to her and, after the initial greetings, Meg saw him grow stiff and tense. He returned to the veranda so that she could also hear what he was telling Beth to do.

'You phone back the cops and say that, yes, there is someone who's an enemy of our family. Someone who might want to harm you, as well as me.' He glanced at Meg and went on. 'His motorbike also fits the one piece of evidence we have. The flash of red and silver that you saw. You'll need to talk to the cops first because it's your case, but then they should call me and I'll fill them in.'

He went back into the garden and talked for some minutes longer, then he ended the call. He returned to the veranda and sat down heavily and in silence.

Meg's anxiety welled up again. 'What is it?'

He sighed, then looked at her. 'A detective called Beth early this morning. 'They've heard from the florist. The order for red roses was placed under a false name, and he gave a fake address.'

'So Beth asking for more roses to be sent probably revealed that?'

'I'd assume so. The police have looked into it further. The call was made from a public phone.'

Meg took this in, and its implications.

He went on. 'The detective asked her if she could think of anyone who might have tried to run her off the road. She couldn't, and she was calling to ask me if by any chance I did. So, I've told her briefly what happened in Vietnam. I said she'd have to leave the share house and she agreed. I'll book her into a motel near the university so she can get to her exams. I've said she shouldn't tell anyone other than her boyfriend where she is. She's packing now.'

'And she didn't question it?'

'Not really. Beth catches on fast. She also didn't want her friends to be at risk if he came looking for her.'

'Should I go home now?'

'I guess so. I'll be on the phone for a while.'

She watched him for a bit longer as he paced back and forth across the backyard. He seemed calm enough to deal with whatever was coming. But as she walked home in the warm sunlight, she had the increasing fear that one of them might actually die.

Colin phoned her several times that day and the next. Phillip Williams had refused to come to the station for an interview and had been arrested on suspicion of dangerous driving, intentionally causing an accident and then leaving the scene. He'd contacted his lawyer, who had then arranged a quick bail hearing. The magistrate had commented that the evidence against Williams was circumstantial so far and that there would need to be more proof. However, one of the bail conditions was that he keep away from Beth and away from Colin's house as well. Colin told Meg all this on the phone in the same measured tones.

'Is that reassuring?' she asked.

'Not really. But at least the cops are aware of it all now.'

'I thought you didn't want them to be.'

'Even if it leads to another hearing about the father's death, I can deal with that now.' He corrected himself. 'Or at least I think I can.'

'So how do you feel?'

He laughed in a dismissive way. 'Okay, but I'm still the real obstacle in all this. If it wasn't for me, if I wasn't here, then you and Beth would both be safe.'

Meg was alarmed. 'So you're going to walk out on us?'

'No.'

But had she heard a slight hesitation in his voice? She wasn't sure. Colin was already saying he had to go and that he'd phone her again soon. Maybe they could meet for breakfast tomorrow.

Meg was still uneasy about what he'd said. It was enough for her to go and check her wardrobe. There was a space at the back where she'd hidden the pentobarbital, the euthanasia drug. She lifted up shoe boxes and pulled clothes off the hanger, looking for the box she kept it in. But it was gone. She closed her eyes – *no, no, no, no!*

She went out to the balcony, the only uncluttered place in the flat, and tried to think it through. Bindi followed her out, and stayed close. Meg considered Nick as a suspect for a moment but then dismissed the thought. Although she'd met families who'd lived through the suicide of a son or daughter, and they'd always said it had been a complete surprise, there was nothing she knew of in Nick's life to even hint at it. No, it must have been Colin who'd taken it. She'd admitted to him that the pentobarbital was hidden in the flat. He must have seen her leave, maybe to meet Jonathan. Then he'd used her hidden key to let himself in and had looked in the obvious places until he found it.

It didn't seem like him to do it, but how well did she really know him? He was dealing with huge stress and had said, perhaps correctly, that she and Beth would be safe if he wasn't there anymore. Maybe he'd decided he had no other option to make them safe. He could go away on his own to an unknown place, but that would still leave her and Beth exposed. She was surer now of his slight hesitation when she'd asked if he was planning to walk out on them. It was enough.

She went back inside and grabbed her phone, then put Leon's hammer in a shopping bag. She might have to break into Colin's house. She checked Bindi's water bowl before she left, and then hurried uphill as fast as she could towards Colin's street. She knocked loudly on the front door and used the doorbell too. There was no sound from inside. She ran around to the back of the house and tried the door to the kitchen. It was locked of course.

She used the hammer to smash a back window. She'd expected his new alarm to sound, but there was only silence inside. She tried to reach through the broken window to try to open the door, but the handle was too far away. She'd have to climb through. She knocked away some of the larger shards of glass that were still wedged in the frame, but she cut herself in several places as she climbed through. Although none of the cuts were very deep, she was dripping blood.

She checked the bedroom first as the most likely place he'd be. From the door she could see that the bed was unmade and the doona piled up as if he could be under it. She was beginning to cry but held back her tears as she pulled the bedding away. He wasn't there. She grabbed some bandages from the bathroom cupboard and searched the rest of the house, but she was already sure that he wasn't there. *Where else? Where else?*

She thought distractedly that they'd even talked about these things, prompted by the piece in *The Atlantic* about dying by the age of seventy-five. She knew Colin would choose somewhere discreet and out of sight of other people. The edge of the river, or the river itself? She had to look. But which way? She turned left and took the path to the golf club because trees and bushes screened it and there were secluded places along the bank. You might take the capsules, then allow yourself to fall unseen into the water as they took hold.

She was red in the face and breathing heavily when she reached the golf club, but there was no sign of Colin. Several people asked if she was okay, but she didn't have the breath to answer them or try to explain. She had to go back. If she had turned left when she should've turned right, and taken the path that led the other way along the river, she knew already that it was probably too late. The tide in the river was flowing out and perhaps Colin's body had already gone with it. She wanted to cry but nothing would come.

She came back to the beginning of the path, still breathing with some difficulty, and looked around at the open stretches of grass. There was still no sign of him. The golf club men had gone and the ibises were back searching for grubs in the grass.

The sheltered place under the road bridge occurred to her. Although the sun was in her eyes, she thought she could see a dark, hunched figure. She walked on as fast as she could towards the bridge – she couldn't run any more – and saw it was indeed Colin. He was sitting on some rocks close to the water that were hidden from the people walking past above him. She staggered on towards him and called out his name. By now he could see that she was in some distress and hurried to meet her.

'What's wrong?'

She managed a gasping breath. 'What are you doing here?'

'Checking in with the king of the river.' He pointed to the pelican, who was in the usual place on the other side. 'What's happened? Is that blood?'

'You didn't go to my flat, did you? You didn't take my pento…' She couldn't finish the question.

He was puzzled and then quietly angry. 'Steal your poison? No, of course I didn't. Why did you ask?'

'Because… Because…' She was already seeing the alternative.

She took her phone out of her pocket with difficulty because of the cuts on her hands and called Nick's number. For once he answered.

'Where are you?' she demanded, relief flooding through her.

'At home. I mean at your place. Bindi's here with me.'

'Stay there.'

'What's wrong? You sound strange. Did the vote go against her?'

She couldn't explain it to him over the phone. 'Just stay there, okay? I'll be back soon.'

Colin pointed to a bench that overlooked the river. 'I think you should sit down for a little while first.'

He helped her to the seat and then suddenly she couldn't hold back the tears. He let her cry.

'Was this about me?' he asked. 'Because I'd said that you and Beth would be safe if I wasn't here?'

She nodded.

'So does that mean you love me?'

She nodded again. It was too hard to speak.

'That's just as well,' he said, 'because I love you too.'

She was finding it hard to stop crying. 'But I broke a window at your place to get in. There's blood everywhere.'

'Did the alarm go off?'

She shook her head.

'I knew that thing was no good.'

She finally stopped crying and looked at him. A sense of great relief was coming over her. Colin was alive and so was Nick. The pelican spread his wings and took off, flying close to the water, down the river towards the sea.

'He takes things easily,' Colin said, 'and he's been here a long time. I'm fond of him.'

It pleased Meg that Colin liked the pelican. Though she would have been happy to stay with him all morning by the river, she knew she couldn't.

'I think I have to go back and talk to Nick.'

He nodded. 'Do you want me there?'

'I don't know.' She made up her mind. 'Yes, I'd like you to come. You might stop me killing him.'

Nick was on the couch with Bindi when they arrived at the flat. He looked up curiously at Meg and her makeshift bandages patched with blood.

She stood in front of him. 'Did you take the capsules from my wardrobe?'

'What capsules?'

She knew he was already hedging. 'You know what capsules. The pentobarbital.'

Nick shrugged. 'I got a good price.'

This in itself alarmed her. 'Who bought them?'

'I think it was for someone…older, though she didn't say so. Yellowjackets are getting harder to get hold of.'

Meg sat down heavily in the armchair. She wondered why she hadn't thought of this as a possibility. Colin stood near the door waiting to see how things would go. She looked up at him and he seemed to understand how she was feeling. He nodded slowly.

Nick was watching her. 'How did you get all those cuts?'

'I had to break a window while I was looking for Colin.'

'Gone missing, had he?'

She ignored this. 'Did you sell anything else?'

'No.'

'And you used it to help pay off the motorbike?'

He didn't answer that. 'But what did you want to keep that stuff for anyway? Do you want to kill yourself?'

'A little more each day.'

'I want you here.' He was sounding quite upset.

'Okay.'

~

In the days that followed, Meg found a kind of peace with Nick that she hadn't felt since he was much younger. She understood that he was who he was and that any attempt she made to change him wouldn't work. She also felt a certain wonder at what was happening between her and Colin. It might be fifty years late, but somehow it could still happen, and it allowed between them a closeness and way of feeling that they didn't have when they were young. Even if there had been no Birthday Ballot and she'd married Colin instead of Leon, it was still not certain that they would've survived all the complexities of life with each other. Nothing much had to be done now other than to embrace the time she and Colin had together until it came to an end.

She knew that Linh had already moved out, and she'd thought of renting the flat for Nick. They'd have more private space and he'd still be nearby. Colin could come to her flat and be there without waiting to see if Nick would arrive. She phoned the agents she knew and the same woman answered. She warned Meg that once it became known the flat was on the market, the golfers would be competing for it. If, after viewing, Meg did want it, then she'd have to move quickly. Meg said she knew the flat and she did want it. She completed an application, but decided to wait for a response before she told Nick. A golfer might still get in first.

There was a knock at the door. Meg looked through the spyhole and saw it was Suzanne. She was probably coming to report on the vote. Meg didn't feel ready for more bad news, but she warily opened the door. Suzanne came in and Bindi, taking her for a friend, went to her in her usual way. Meg waited tensely. If the vote was against them, whatever she or Jonathan could do might not change anything. The rules were made by the majority and would be enforced. She had another wayward thought about kidnapping Suzanne's cat, but then, for almost the first time since she'd met her, she saw that Suzanne was smiling.

'She's allowed to stay.'

'What? Is she?'

Suzanne was clearly pleased with herself. 'It was going against you, but then two late answers came in from residents who were on your side and there was a tie. I had the casting vote.' She leaned down and rubbed the little dog's head. 'I like her too.'

Meg sighed with relief. 'Thank you for that.'

Susanne left, and Meg when to sit out on the balcony with Bindi beside her. It was a real relief that there was to be no further dispute over the little dog. But, as she sat there, more thoughts about Phillip Williams, and what he'd told her in his calm and reasonable voice about the shooting of his father, began to intrude. What he'd repeated to her, she thought, could have been said to a kid in his teens who'd begun to look for answers about his father's death. Young Phillip Williams would have believed what he'd been told back then. He probably still did. Did he cling to it as something that made sense of his own life and gave it a cold but certain purpose?

Something else troubled her. Had she been wrong in thinking that, once there were more eyes on him, Phillip Williams would leave Colin alone? Had her confident intrusions, based on this certainty, been entirely wrong? She didn't believe that Williams' version of his father's death was accurate, but she still felt she should tell Colin what he'd said.

In the peaceful days that followed, she convinced herself that she didn't have to raise it with him yet. There were other things to think about.

21

Meg was sitting with Colin on his back veranda after breakfast on a warm quiet morning when they heard a motorbike revving loudly.

Colin said, 'It must be him. But he won't try anything in daylight.'

There was a heavy knocking on the front door. It was loud enough to be the police, although of course it wasn't. Colin stood up as if to go and answer it.

Meg was shocked. 'What are you doing?'

'I'm going out to talk to him. He won't do anything.'

'I wouldn't be so sure of that…'

Meg followed him along the hall, then turned aside to the window that was nearest to the front door, being careful not to move the curtain. From there she could see a figure in a motorbike helmet and black clothes standing on the first of the five steps, and the words 'the angel of death' occurred to her. She could hear Colin already unlocking the door.

She remained by the window, hoping he was right and Williams wouldn't do anything during the day. But, at the same time, she felt a crushing sense of dread. The window was open at the bottom and she could hear Colin speaking.

He said, 'Take off your helmet and talk to me. Show me your face.'

Williams had stayed on the bottom step. 'Not with your new cameras.'

Colin's voice grew harder. 'This ends now. It's been too long, and now you're terrorising people I love.'

'Then you have to drop this shit with the cops. If not, I'll…'

'You'll what?'

Colin took a sudden step back, and Meg saw that Willams was holding a gun. She stifled a scream, and turned away from the window. As quietly as she could, she went to her medical bag, which was still on a chair near the front door, and took out Leon's hammer. She let herself out the back door, then ran as silently as she could along the side of the house in her rubber-soled shoes.

She took one quick glance around the corner. Colin was now on the top step, which meant he had been edging away from the house, towards the gun. Phillip Williams was on the bottom step, and he still had his helmet on with the visor down. He wasn't moving or speaking. She saw the reason. A mother and a girl of about six had stopped to speak to an older woman on the footpath outside the house next door.

Meg could hear Williams speaking to Colin, keeping his voice low because of the people in the street.

'Go back into the house.'

'No.'

The gun was in Williams' right hand and she could see that his body hid it from the people in the street. Meg thought of calling out to them, but Williams had already come this far – he was capable of anything. There was no time. These women and the little girl couldn't help now. And, if Meg called out, it might startle Williams and the gun could go off.

She gripped the handle of the hammer and tried to stop her hands shaking. She took a slow, deep breath as she began edging along the narrow space behind the lemon trees, making her way closer to the street. She kept low, hoping that Williams wouldn't see her because he was looking up the stairs towards Colin. She saw Colin's eyes flick to one side – this meant he had seen her through the leaves. He was telling her to keep away. But she went on, edging closer, hoping that the motorbike helmet would make it harder for Williams to hear her approaching. She kept going until she was crouched behind the tree closest to him.

There was a moment when he turned his head slightly, and she thought he'd seen her, but he was only glancing at the small group on the footpath. The women had finished talking and were walking away. The little girl had noticed Meg crouching behind the lemon tree, and she looked back as her mother led her away.

Now, with any witnesses gone, there was no time left. Meg knew what she had to do. She leapt towards Williams and raised the hammer high. He stepped back and turned the gun towards her. Meg screamed as she swung the big hammer as hard as she could, and brought it down on his right shoulder. She heard the cracking of bone and the heavy sound of metal falling onto the stairs. She raised the hammer and brought it down again.

He cried out in pain and tried to reach for the gun with his other hand. Meg swung the hammer again, connecting with the side of his helmet. The black visor cracked and clattered to the ground as Williams slipped and fell. She dropped the hammer and quickly grabbed the gun. She turned the barrel towards him, and backed away into a space between the lemon trees as he climbed to his feet. Colin came down the stairs, but he made sure he didn't get between her and Williams.

Although Meg was holding the gun, she knew she couldn't fire it. Williams seemed to know this too. He looked at her with a mix of pain and fury. Her first thought was to give the gun to Colin. But what if he used it? This could only make things also worse. She looked up between the leaves of the lemon tree and then, almost by instinct, threw the gun high into the air so that it landed on the corrugated-iron roof of the house.

It landed high on the roof, then began to slide back down. She held her breath, hoping it was small enough to catch in the gutter. There was a shocked pause while the three of them listened to it slowly sliding downwards until it lodged in the gutter with the barrel sticking out over the edge.

Colin came further down the stairs and made a move to pull off Williams' helmet. The two men wrestled with each other, but it looked like Williams couldn't raise his right arm. This meant Colin was able to get the helmet off him.

Meg looked up at the security cameras and thought – *please be working.*

Colin said, 'The cameras just recorded all that.'

'Fuck you. This isn't over.' Williams looked at Meg. 'And fuck you too, doctor. And your son.'

She watched him as he went to his motorbike. He managed to climb onto it, although he was clearly struggling with the pain in his arm. The engine roared and he was gone.

She and Colin looked along the street. They were silent, there was nothing to say. It felt like the shock of what happened was only just sinking in. The scent of the lemon trees seemed to grow stronger and she winced as she remembered the sound of hammer and the cracking of bone in his shoulder. Then she heard a crashing, grating sound before a splintering impact. She and Colin ran out onto the street and saw Williams' motorbike on its side at the intersection. Then she saw another motorbike – it was Nick's.

'*Oh no, no, no, no, no!*' she cried out.

She yelled at Colin to get her medical bag and began running. She reached the mess of motorbikes at the intersection and hurried to Nick. He was lying on his side. The leather of his jacket was torn open, but he'd raised the visor on his helmet, and she could see he was conscious. He was muttering, 'Shit. Shit. Shit.' She looked across at Williams. He was lying very still on his back with his neck bent sideways. His head was in the gutter where the two streets met – no helmet.

She looked back down at her son. 'Don't you fucking move! You hear me? *Don't try to move!*'

Nick went on muttering, 'Shit, shit, shit,' to himself while she stepped towards Williams.

She felt for a pulse – *nothing*. She pushed her fingers into his mouth, feeling for obstructions. She looked back at Nick. For once, he was doing what he was told, staying still, but she could see the gentle rise and fall of his chest. And then, as if on autopilot, she interlocked her fingers and began chest compressions, trying to resuscitate the man who had just come to Colin's house to kill him. She counted out loud. 'One, two, three, four, five, six, seven, eight…'

Somewhere behind her, she could hear Colin talking on his phone. 'Yes, two ambulances… Yes, she's a doctor and she's doing resuscitation.' He gave the address. 'We'll need the police as well.'

Meg breathed twice into Williams' mouth, then restarted her count of compressions on his chest. She could taste blood, and she knew it wasn't hers.

She saw Colin's shoes beside her and glanced up. He had a confused look on his face, almost as though he didn't understand what she was doing. Again she breathed twice into Williams' mouth, interlocked her fingers, and used her bodyweight to compress his chest. 'One, two, three, four…'

She could feel the beginnings of fatigue, but she continued. She couldn't ask Colin to take over. Then at last she heard a siren approaching and two male paramedics arrived. One took over the resuscitation while the other checked for a pulse.

She went back to Nick. Colin was sitting on the road beside him. A police car arrived, and a policewoman approached and asked Colin if he knew the motorcyclist they were trying to resuscitate.

'Yes.'

'Is he a friend of yours?'

'No. But we know who he is.'

'What about his next of kin? They say he wasn't wearing a helmet.'

'That's right. He wasn't. I don't know about his next of kin, but I know his name – Phillip Williams. And I can get you his address too.'

The policewoman shook her head sadly and walked away.

Meg placed a reassuring hand on Nick's shoulder, but she was careful not to move him. He looked up at her, his eyes drooping. 'I feel sleepy.'

'You have to stay awake!'

'Are you angry with me?'

'Just don't go to sleep.'

Another ambulance with two more paramedics arrived, a man and a woman. Meg told them she was Nick's mother and a doctor. They checked him over, then carefully moved him onto a spinal board. They agreed to let Meg ride with him in the back of the ambulance and the female paramedic got in with her.

'Do you know how it happened?' she asked.

'No.'

~

At the hospital Nick was admitted and then taken away for head and spinal scans. Meg found a seat in the waiting room, which was painted a bright white with soothing landscapes on the walls. She remembered the time when hospital walls were painted green on the bottom half and brown on top. Or was it the other way around? Whatever it was, those days were long gone. The friends and families of other patients sat around the edge of the room in small groups. The adults had tense expressions while the children wriggled and asked for more chips.

Meg knew well enough that hospital waiting rooms were places where minutes stretched out the longest. She tried to settle herself, but the last few hours were taking a toll. Her heart was still beating fast and she knew her blood pressure would be high. She wondered if she should ask one of the nurses to test it, but they were busy and would probably send her down to the emergency room. No, she would stay where she was and wait.

Her own blood-pressure machine was in her medical bag at the accident site, although Colin would've taken it to his place once the ambulances left. At least if she had a stroke she was already in a hospital. She tried to calm her breathing, watching the slow movement of a clock on the wall.

Her phone, which was in another pocket, vibrated as a call came in. It was Colin and she went out into the corridor to talk to him.

'Nick may be all right,' she told him. 'Do you know anything about Williams?'

Colin took his time to answer. 'He didn't make it. The ambos said his head hit that point on the kerb where the footpaths intersect.'

Meg shuddered and again thought – *no helmet*. He'd probably died quickly, she thought, because there wasn't much blood, only that trickle from his mouth as she'd worked on him. She still had the faint taste of it, although she'd tried to wash it out when she got to the hospital. She was slow to answer Colin, still conscious of her own rapid heartbeat, and he waited for her.

It was hard to speak but she managed it. 'Are you relieved?'

He didn't answer the question. 'The police will want to talk to Nick about how it happened.'

'It's plain enough, isn't it? Williams was speeding. He ignored the stop sign and he was riding without a helmet.'

If Colin had any doubts, he didn't raise them. 'Yes, it's plain enough. Do you want me to come to the hospital?'

'Not yet.'

The silence between them lengthened, and they ended the call. She went back to the waiting room.

More time passed, then a nurse came for her and took her up in the lift and along a passageway to an ordinary ward. Nick was propped up against the pillows. This meant his neck was all right. His shoulder was in a sling. He looked very pale but more or less normal.

He seemed surprised to see her. 'Were you waiting all this time?'

'Yes, of course I was.'

'It took a while before they finished the tests and got me sorted. My collarbone's broken and they had to set that. But the helmet did what it's meant to do. Break your collarbone instead of your neck.'

He sounded almost proud of this and as if it proved the correctness of his trust in motorbikes.

'What about concussion?'

'They don't think it's too bad.'

'Did you have a headache? Do you feel sick?'

'Yeah. A bad headache and I threw up. But they said I should be out of here in a day or so.'

She answered very flatly. 'You were lucky.'

'I was.'

She looked away.

'What is it, Mum?'

She looked around to make sure they were really alone, then kept her voice low. 'Did you know it was him?'

Nick looked at her but said nothing.

She asked another question. 'Did you recognise the sound of his engine?'

'He ran the stop sign.'

'But could you have avoided him?'

'Why wasn't he wearing a helmet? He should've had a helmet on.'

She said it again in almost a whisper. 'I asked you whether you could have avoided him.'

He looked back at her. His eyelids were sinking, nearly closed. 'Are you sure you want to know?'

She didn't respond. Whether she'd wanted him to or not, he had answered her question.

He asked, 'Did you see it? The actual crash?'

'No.'

'So why do you think…?'

She cut him off. 'I'm trying not to think anything really. He was riding with a broken collarbone. He probably couldn't control the…'

'What do you mean? His collarbone was already broken? How do you know?'

'I hit him with Dad's hammer.'

'*You what?*'

The hospital curtain was pulled back suddenly, startling them both. Meg half-expected to hear a voice telling her that all they'd just said had been recorded. But it was only a male nurse coming to do the routine checks on Nick. Then a doctor came and told Nick they'd got the scans back. It was okay for him to sleep.

22

A taxi dropped Meg outside her flat, but she knew as she started towards the door that she didn't want to be there on her own. She needed to be with Colin. She collected Bindi from the flat and clicked on her lead. They walked slowly up the hill towards Colin's house. He must have heard the sound of the gate opening, and he came out to meet them. They held each other, not speaking, while Bindi sniffed around the lemon trees.

Then Colin looked up at the gun that was still in the roof gutter. 'It's different to a helicopter, but I think you've saved my life now too.'

'I guess we're even. Did you tell the police about it? I mean about him coming here with the gun and the rest of it?'

'I kept it pretty broad, but I think they're leaving it at that. I hope so anyway. I checked the stupid security cameras, but they'd turned themselves off again. The guy's giving me a refund.' He turned towards the house and Meg and Bindi followed. 'How's Nick?'

'He'll be all right, but only because he was wearing a helmet.' She wasn't ready to tell Colin what Nick had said at the hospital.

Meg led Bindi through the house, past the little table where her medical bag with Leon's hammer had been, and then out to the back veranda. Colin made coffee, and she was glad to sit in the late sun and look out while Bindi inspected the fallen leaves around the gum trees.

Colin handed her a cup. 'The police told me he had two sons. They've arranged for his body to be released for cremation.'

'Are they going to come after you now?'

'I hope not. But I got the private investigator to check on them just in case. Neither of them ended up in the army.'

'So they still have their sanity?'

He laughed. 'I know. I'm working on it. And not just for you.'

He raised his coffee cup and she felt tears in her eyes as they clinked their mugs together. She said, 'The forecast says the rain's starting again tomorrow. Should we take Bindi for a walk?'

She noticed that Colin pulled the door closed but didn't lock it. The three of them went up the hill, then over the ridge and down through the golf course where the strips of exposed earth from her car accident had been covered by turf that was slowly taking root.

'Do you think it was him who drained out my brake fluid?' Meg asked.

He considered this. 'I think your mechanic may be right and it can't be proved either way but…'

'But given that we know he did come after Beth and that I was also an obvious target…'

'Yes, I think we can probably assume it was him. We know he couldn't just cut your brake cables. That would've been obvious to the police.'

'And he was never obvious, was he? Except at the end when he came with that gun. But then even the gun was discrete.' She paused. 'What are you going to do about it? I don't think you can leave it up there. Someone might see it.'

'Unlikely but, yes, I agree.'

'So what will you do with it?'

'Don't worry, I'm not going to sell it on the internet.'

They walked by the river, and then headed back to Colin's place.

Meg sat on the veranda with Bindi. Colin dug a hole beside the trunk of one of the gum trees and then went down the side of the house with a ladder. The sun was dipping almost to the west, disappearing now and then behind tomorrow's grey clouds. He returned with something wrapped in black plastic and began to bury it in a hole he'd dug under the biggest white gum.

Meg walked down to watch. 'Are you sure it's a good idea to keep it here? On your property?'

'I'm not going anywhere.'

~

Nick was released from hospital a few days later. He'd been told he must stay quiet while he recovered from the after-effects of concussion. His arm and shoulder would be in a sling for about six weeks. The doctors had told him it was a bad break and would take time to heal.

They sat on the balcony in silence at first, then he said, 'The police have released my motorbike. It can be picked up any time.'

'Does that mean they're no longer investigating the…?'

'Accident? No, they're not. Or at least not as far as I know. They did come and talk to me though.'

'What did you tell them?'

'That I don't remember much.'

'No, I guess you wouldn't.'

He turned to look at her. 'You don't want me to… complicate things, do you?'

She shook her head. The key facts were indisputable. Williams had ridden at full speed through a stop sign without a helmet.

They said nothing for a few minutes. There were no golfers and Meg could hear the wind in the casuarinas near the river.

Nick looked out at them. 'I love that sound.'

'So do I. It's because they don't have leaves, only the thin green stems that are actually tiny branches. They move together in the wind and hush like that. Branchlets, they're called.'

He looked at her narrowly. 'So am I a branchlet of you?'

'I suppose so.'

'Just not worth as much as a casuarina though?'

This got to her. 'Oh, Nick… That's just not true.'

She'd said this with an emphasis she hoped might convince him to believe it. What had brought her to this place by the golf course had initially been her anger with him, and now she could barely remember what she'd been angry about.

'I'm glad the casuarinas are there. I like this place.'

Meg was pleased to hear it but she didn't want to raise the possibility of Linh's flat with him yet. She needed to know first that she could get it.

Instead she asked, 'Did the police say anything about your motorbike?'

'They said it's a write-off but that I might be able to salvage a few parts.'

'Was it insured?'

'No. That was going to cost too much.'

Meg thought about this. 'One thing I'm not going to do is buy you another motorbike. Not after…' She stopped.

'Okay then, I suppose I'll have to switch to Dad's car.'

She was pleased and relieved. It felt to her like he was finally growing up. Nick smiled as if he knew what she was thinking, then he seemed to feel some pain in the small of his back. He shifted uncomfortably.

'Are you all right?' she asked. 'Do you need a painkiller?'

He gave her a wry look. 'Have you got any ice?'

She looked at him.

He grinned happily as if he'd caught her out. 'I mean the cold stuff in the freezer.'

She laughed. 'I've got that. Not the other stuff.'

She headed for the kitchen to get it, looking at the couch and the armchair on the way. When she'd bought them, she was imagining that she'd be mostly on her own and so they'd remain clean and white, or off-white, for the rest of her time there. But Nick and Bindi between them had certainly aged the couch and there were faint bloodstains on the armchair from that terrible hour or so when she was searching for Colin. They both testified to how different her life would have been if she'd stayed on her expected path. If she and Colin hadn't found each other again. If Nick had moved to the first flat and not come back. If Bindi hadn't been rescued. Her life had changed and expanded in these last weeks and months. The couch and the armchair were a small sacrifice.

She stayed in her flat looking after Nick and heard nothing more from Colin. She thought at first that he might be staying away out of concern for Nick. That seemed to make sense, but as the days passed – three days, four – she became increasingly troubled. She began to feel that she must somehow make it work again between them soon or it might disintegrate altogether. She didn't know if that was already happening. On the fifth day she simply picked up the phone and called him.

When he answered, she asked briskly, 'Can we meet?'

'Where?'

'By the river.'

'Okay. When?'

'Now?'

'Okay.'

She couldn't judge anything from his tone. She realised she hadn't prepared for this and was wearing baggy old jeans that she had meant to throw out, but she couldn't stop to change. She called out to Nick, who was on the balcony with Bindi, to say she was going out for a while, then she left and headed for the river. Colin must have done much the same because they met near the bottom of the slope.

They continued in silence towards the river and as they approached the bank, Meg noticed the broken tree branches and ruptured earth caused by the helicopter crash. No-one had yet got around to dealing with it. It wasn't on the fairway so perhaps no-one cared. They stood together looking out at the water flowing past and neither of them spoke.

It was Colin who broke the silence. 'Has it changed?' he asked without looking at her.

It was a strangely critical question for Meg. She answered it carefully. 'No. Have you?'

'Have I changed?'

'Yes.'

'In what way?'

'In any way?'

He seemed to recognise that his answer was important to her. 'We've both been through a lot.'

She treated this as hedging. 'You think I don't know that?'

'Look at me,' he said, and she did. 'I know a lot's happened but there's one thing that hasn't changed through it all and it's that I love you.'

She just looked at him. 'Yes.'

'What does yes mean?'

'That I love you too.'

They said nothing for a little while as they watched the river. The tide was flowing inland.

'Why do you love me?' he asked at length.

'I've known you since we were thirteen. I know you.'

'That's not an answer. I'm different now. A different person.'

She thought about it. 'There are changes, yes, but you're still who you are.'

'And you love that person?'

'Unfortunately, yes.'

'Why unfortunately?'

She thought again for a moment before she answered. 'Because at this stage of life you're expected to move quietly. Not stir up the air or the water, not do anything foolish like falling in love. That belongs to the generations below us. They own love now, or at least they think they do.'

He laughed. 'If you're sure. Then I guess we'll prove them wrong?'

'I'm sure.'

They stood together and watched the tide as it continued to flow inland. Although it was steadily retreating from the sea, it seemed to Meg that it was flowing the right way.

ACKNOWLEDGEMENTS

My special thanks go to my son, Jack Ellis, who edited the book and helped me all the way through with ideas. He is a good writer himself, and he generously gave me his time and also his patient and excellent thoughts. My thanks, and love, go especially to him.

I'd also like to thank my professional editor, Simone Ford. She was always right in her comments and corrections, and she made a significant difference. I'm very grateful too for her patience and her help.

My warm thanks also to Jane O'Keefe to whom the book is dedicated, and who proofread the final draft with the care and kindness that she always freely gives. I'd also like to acknowledge and thank Meredith Burgmann for the reference I used to her funny story about being charged for obstructing access to the men's lavatory at a Vietnam War rally.

Apart from the people who made this book possible, my thanks also go to Marrickville, my new home, and to the landscape and creatures of the Cooks River. I feel like they were always at my side as I wrote this book.

Anne Ellis - August 2024 - Marrickville

ABOUT THE AUTHOR

Anne Brooksbank was born in Melbourne and graduated with an MA in History and English Literature from Melbourne University. She also studied painting at the National Gallery School. She has written eight novels, including *On Loan, Archer, All My Love, Mother's Day* and *Marriage Acts*. Her novel, *Father's Day*, was shortlisted for the Prime Minister's Literary Awards in 2012. She has also written extensively for film and television and has won six Australian Writers Guild Awards (AWGIEs).

She has three children and two grandchildren. She lives in Sydney, Australia.

www.ingramcontent.com/pod-product-compliance
Lightning Source LLC
Chambersburg PA
CBHW031259120726
47906CB00003B/812